Potomac Review

Potomac Review

EDITOR IN CHIEF
JULIE WAKEMAN-LINN

POETRY EDITOR
KATHERINE SMITH

FICTION EDITOR
JOHN W. WANG

ADMINISTRATIVE ASSISTANT/WEBMASTER
OM B. RUSTEN

ASSOCIATE EDITORS

DIANE BOSSER	DAVID LOTT
KENNETH FLEMING	MIKE MAGGIO
COURTNEY FORD	DAVID SAITZEFF
LISA FRIEDMAN	JESSIE SEIGEL
ROBERT GIRON	MARIANNE SZLYK
ALBERT KAPIKIAN	KAROLINA WILK
MICHAEL LANDWEBER	SHERRI WOOSLEY
MICHAEL LEBLANC	HANANAH ZAHEER

INTERNS
COLLIN BROWN
RYAN BROWN
MORENIKE ROSSMAN
TETYANA RUDENKO
JACK STUTZ

Published by the Paul Peck Humanities Institute at
Montgomery College, Rockville
51 Mannakee Street, Rockville, MD 20850

Potomac Review has been made possible through
the generosity of Montgomery College.

A special thanks to Dean Rodney Redmond.

For submission guidelines and more information:
www.potomacreview.org

Potomac Review, Inc. is a not-for-profit 501 c(3) corp.
Member, Council of Literary Magazines & Presses
Indexed by the American Humanities Index
ISBN: 978-0999040300
ISSN:10073 – 1989

SUBSCRIBE TO *POTOMAC REVIEW*
One year at $24 (2 issues)
Two years at $36 (4 issues)
Sample copy order, $10 (Single issue)

Cover photo from Creative Commons
Cover and interior design by Carol Chu

TABLE OF CONTENTS

FICTION

Marian Crotty | WHAT COUNTS AS LOVE | 1

Søren G. Palmer | DISCIPLES, SOLDIERS AND KINGS | 23

Robert P. Kaye | PICKUP BALL IN THE PARKING LOT OF

HEAVENLY DELIGHTS | 50

Mary Taugher | HOWARD'S END | 64

Richard Farrell | HOSTILE ADVANCES | 110

Julia Tagliere | USEFUL THINGS | 125

Mary Grimm | COMPANY | 148

Matthew Socia | EMBARGOES | 167

NONFICTION

Zlatina G. Sandalska | TAKING NOTES | 29

Liz Prato | DESCENDANT(S) | 87

Sue Eisenfeld | TAKING IT | 138

POETRY

Kareem Tayyar | THE STREET MUSICIAN | 20

Sandra Kohler | HOT BATHS | 21

Matt Farrell | FOURTH OF JULY ON THE AMERICAN RIVER |27

Donelle Dreese | ALL THE BREATHLESS PEOPLE OF THE SUN | 28

Joe Cottonwood | BIRTHNIGHT | 47

E. Laura Golberg | SHAVER | 49

Alex Andrew Hughes | SWITCH-BLADE NAMES | 61

Richard Peabody | SPARE CHANGE | 63

Joseph Zaccardi | THE BLIND | 83

       | IN THE VALLEY OF WINDOWS | 84

Charlotte Pence | DNA REFLECTS ON DEATH | 85

Andrea Potos | MORNING OF MY 56TH BIRTHDAY | 107

       | HER LAST HOUR | 108

Joanne Rocky Delaplaine | CHINCOTEAGUE | 109

Sean Sam | ANOTHER MORNING | 121

Lynn McGee | JUPITER AND CHAPARRAL | 123

Lucien Darjeun Meadows | TIRESIAS | 133

Melanie Henderson | THE WOODEATERS | 135

       | HOW TO KEEP GOING | 137

Raymond Philip Asaph | EVEN IN THE JUNK YARD | 144

Samantha Leigh Futhey | DRIVING IN IOWA, EAST ON

       HIGHWAY 30 | 145

       | FARMALL | 147

Richard Jones | THE EGG | 161

       | BLUE STARS | 162

       | THE SUITCASE | 164

Afua Ansong | THE GIRLS WITH THE ISSUE OF BLOOD |

       | WOMAN: BECOMING | 166

AUTHOR BIOS | 175

WHAT COUNTS AS LOVE

MARIAN CROTTY

When the swelling went down, and she could almost see straight again, Karleen got a job as a carpenter's assistant at Mint Hill Construction, sweeping up debris and helping the skilled laborers with whatever they needed. The job site in East Charlotte was a midrange condo development sandwiched between a wooded neighborhood of narrow houses and an empty parking lot with a faded banner that promised a Target Shopping Center was coming soon. Two condos were finished and several others framed, but most of the site was composed of large, flattened-out mounds of red clay marked with wooden stakes.

It was not far from the duplex where she'd been staying with her sister, Mandy, and her husband, David, sleeping on an air mattress in the small yellow room that would soon belong to their baby. Her sister's neighborhood was just forty minutes away from the lake house she'd shared with JT, but it might as well have been a different universe. Instead of boats and water skis, tires, rental signs, and rusty disemboweled cars cluttered the lawns.

On her first day, she parked on the street behind a mud-splattered pickup truck, waited twenty minutes until exactly

five before six, and then walked across the red clay to the alumi-
num trailer, where Abe had told her to meet him. The air was
cold against her bare arms, but she knew she'd soon be sweat-
ing. Three Hispanic men stood by the side of the trailer, talk-
ing in Spanish and holding large plastic thermoses that looked
more like buckets. When she passed them, their eyes watched
her walk up the steps, knock on the door, and slip inside.

Abe was wearing a navy-blue Mint Hill Construction shirt
with his name on a patch. His long gray ponytail was sec-
tioned off with multicolored rubber bands. She'd never met
him before, but like everybody else at the church she went to
with Mandy and David, he'd seen her name on the prayer list
and wanted to help. He shook her hand a little too hard and
gestured to a metal folding chair across from a particle board
workstation holding an old desktop computer and a large plas-
tic tub of Winn-Dixie brand Cheetos. He copied down her
driver's license number and told her to bring a photocopy of
it and her social security card. Then he went over the safety
procedures, which he said included not just the hard hat and
goggles but the good sense to pay attention all the time, no
matter what.

He led her across the clay lot and past the men in tank tops
and frayed jeans congregating in the garage of one of the fin-
ished condos, which was filled with lumber and power tools.

He showed her a rusted wheelbarrow, a large metal dustpan
and a broom with thick bristles curved into an L.

"Don't take too much at once," he said. "You'll want to at
first, but you'll be working a long day, and you'll tire out."

By the time the sun had come up, the workers had divided

into crews and were spread out across the site. As soon as she swept up one building and hauled the load to the dumpster, the floor of the next was covered with nails, screws, and plastic water bottles. No one bothered with trashcans or bags, but the floors had to stay clean so the men who walked around on metal drywall stilts, which looked like a combination between crutches and pogo sticks, didn't trip.

By eight o'clock and the first break, she had sunscreen in her eyes and a U of sweat around her sports bra. The space between her shoulder blades ached, and the meat of her palms was pink and sore. A young roofer with quad muscles so thick she could see them through his jeans came over to the trailer where she was leaning into the shade and trying to avoid a conversation. He handed her a half-frozen bottle of Gatorade.

"You don't stay hydrated, your legs will lock up on you," he said, in a Kentucky accent. "It's a long day out here, and it only gets hotter."

Karleen took the bottle and swallowed a sip of sweet-salt slush.

"I'm Avery," he said, winking. "Probably I saved your life." He continued, "I mean, that's worth one date at least. Don't you think?"

She crossed her arms so he wouldn't see her nipples under her sweaty shirt. "No."

Avery shrugged. "I'll give you time to get to know me," he said. "Women love me. You'll see."

Karleen laughed. "I'll bet."

Avery licked his cloudy teeth, which were pink with Gatorade. "A summer romance for a summer job," he said. "Isn't that how it works?"

May was not yet over, and she hadn't thought past the end of the week, let alone the end of the summer, but she found herself shaking her head. "This isn't for the summer," she said. "This is my job now."

"You better learn something other than cleanup, then," he said. "The crew gets real small after summer when the work slows down."

Karleen was twenty. Outside of the year at Taco Bell when she was seventeen, she had never had a job. She'd thought she might become a hairdresser after high school, but then she'd met JT, who said he didn't see why she needed a job in addition to taking care of him, which was hard enough. He was twenty-four and the youth group leader at the church where she'd grown up. The other kids liked him because he could imitate the way Pastor Anderson's face shook when he preached and because he brought in posters and tickets from TriStar Motorsports, where he did marketing, but Karleen was drawn to his vulnerability. She saw the flicker of sadness that always flashed across his face after a joke, and this is how she knew he needed her.

She'd had sex with her junior-year prom date the year before she'd met JT, but JT wouldn't sleep with her until she turned eighteen and was old enough for them to get married at the courthouse. He told her she was a born-again virgin now that she was taking church and God seriously and that their wedding night would be the real first time she had sex.

For the first few months, JT complimented the recipes she taught herself from *Bon Appétit* and the way the granite counters and hardwood floors gleamed. When they argued, the issue was always her high school friends and whether she was keeping up with them so she could talk to the prom date. So she hid her prom pictures at Mandy's house and saw her friends only in the afternoons when he was at the office. One Sunday she wore her hair up in a barrette for church and, when Pastor Anderson shook her hand at the door, he told her she looked beautiful.

JT was silent in the car, but when they got home he said, "How long have you been screwing him?"

Karleen poked him in the chest and laughed. "You're jealous of a sixty-year-old?" she said. "That's pathetic."

His face was red, and she knew exactly how pissed off he was, but she didn't stop.

"If I were going to screw somebody," she said, "it would be the choir director, because he's hot."

And that's when JT punched her in the ribs and left a disk of swollen tissue just above her lungs.

After work, Karleen found Abe on the far side of the dirt lot, loading his tools into the back of his truck. On the window of the cab was a bumper sticker with a picture of a revolver that said, "I Don't Dial 911."

"I have a big favor to ask," she said.

He looked at her fingers, which were worrying a blister.

"You aren't quitting on me, are you?" He squinted at her but kept his eyes warm, and she wondered what all he knew. Behind him, the framers were moving the lumber back to the garage, where it could be locked up for the night. One of them had the same buzzed hair and bowlegged strut as a friend of JT's she'd met once at a bar. She couldn't be sure if he was the same guy, but the sight of him made the blood drain from her face.

"If I could learn to frame," she said. "I'd be able to work year-round, right?"

Most of the men were shirtless or down to a sweat-soaked wife-beater, but Abe still had on his work shirt.

"I'm good with directions," she said. "And I have tools." She was thinking of the starter toolkit she had spent the weekend assembling from second-hand stores and garage sales. She could hear the eagerness in her own voice, and it made her cheeks burn.

Abe pushed his fingers through the scruff on his chin. "You wouldn't rather do office work in the long run?" he said. "Something'll open up at the warehouse if you're patient."

She shook her head and made herself keep his gaze until he looked down at the bed of his truck.

"Okay," he said finally. "You start coming in an hour early off the clock, and I'll get you started."

In the mornings, with the streetlights still on and the sky starting to pink, she helped him inventory the day's materials. He showed her how to cut studs and calculate the pitch of a roof, stood beside her, guiding her hands as she made looping cuts with a coping saw. At night, after work, Karleen read *Blueprint Reading for the Construction Trades,* a dog-eared manual from the 1960s she'd picked up at the public library, and quizzed herself on terms like "common American Bond" and "queen post."

Her body began to toughen—her forearm muscles fattening, her back broadening, thick calluses forming where the blisters had healed. She'd thought the saws would scare her, but she liked the way the vibrations shivered through her arms and legs, the way her heart picked up when the blade began to whir. If she wasn't careful, she could slice her hand open, and the rush of this focus—her mind still and quiet against the spray of sawdust—thrilled her.

At the police station, she asked Shanda, the victim's advocate, what would happen to JT, and she shrugged. She was a big woman in a clingy nylon dress who always seemed tired and out of breath. The last time Karleen had seen JT, he'd broken the orbital bone on the left side of her face. She'd had surgery to remove the bone fragments from her eye socket, but her left eye was slightly lower than her right, and when she looked directly above her, the world went double. JT had been charged with strangulation and serious injury, but he was out on bail, a release conditional upon his keeping the terms of the restraining order she'd filed against him.

"Could be probation," Shanda said. "Could be a couple years in prison."

The room was empty except for a police academy calendar and a poster of a dusty purple peony in a black plastic frame. Like all the police officers and social workers Karleen had encountered, Shanda had constructed an office that wouldn't give any clues about who she was.

Karleen swallowed. "He tried to kill me."

"I'm with you," Shanda said. "I am, but if he gets probation, you might be safer." With probation, she explained, JT would live close by but would have three years of monitoring and could practice fighting the urge to come hurt her, knowing if he did, he'd go back to prison. "Prison is different," she said. "With prison, he sits in there a couple years, thinking about how much he wants to kill you, and then they set him free."

Karleen massaged the tightness forming between her shoulders. "Will he go to trial?" she said, wondering if he still hated her and what it would be like to see him.

Shanda tapped a teal green fingernail on the desk. "Let's hope not."

In the afternoons, when David was still at the auto shop, Karleen and Mandy drank coffee and shared articles from the *Charlotte Observer*. Karleen kept it light—mocking the stupid questions people sent to Billy Graham, like, "Is it in God's plan for me to cheat on my husband?" or, "Is my child misbehaving because he is possessed?" But Mandy liked reading from the crime news so she could say things like, "Being in the church won't keep you away from evil, but it puts you close to God, and being close to him is the only thing that helps anyone."

Because she'd met JT in church, Karleen knew Mandy worried she'd given up on God and religion, but Mandy had it wrong. Karleen needed forgiveness now more than ever. The fact that her eyesight was probably damaged forever or that she had a jagged half-moon scar on her ribs was not just proof of JT's cruelty, but also a testament to Karleen's guilt—a memory of what the two of them had counted as love.

Many things she would never tell her sister. For instance, Karleen had often provoked JT on purpose. He'd always given her a warning that he would hurt her, always said, "You stop it Karleen," or, "If you don't back off, I'm going to lose it," but she still said whatever she thought would hurt him most, the exchange she made for the punch he'd land on her stomach, where the black bruise could stay hidden. He'd apologize, telling her, "I love you too much. Thinking about losing you makes me crazy," and they'd cling to each other like accident victims and have the kind of sex that made the whole room spin.

The second to last fight, the day before he stomped on her face, he told her that no one else would put up with someone like her, that no one else in the world could love her, and so she drank with a friend and went home with a stranger. She had meant this to be a private rebellion, but when she came home the next morning, JT was waiting for her in the living room, with her blue cashmere sweater poised on his lap between her pinking shears.

"Did letting some asshole fuck you make you feel like hot shit," he said, his old complaint that had never been true until now. He cut off a sleeve of her sweater and let it rest on the leg of his boxers. "You think he knows your name? You think he gives a fuck what your face looks like?"

His face was puffy and red, and the room smelled like cigarettes, but he was sober. He sat at the coffee table, covered in a collection of fast food wrappers, put his hand down his boxers and started touching himself. He stared her down, willing her to watch him, and in that moment in the dirty living room with blue fabric strewn across his lap and a concerted effort between his eyebrows, he seemed pathetic and childish, a person who deserved to be hurt.

"You know," she said. "I *did* have fun last night. He had a big dick, and I had a good orgasm, and we might have dinner next weekend."

In July, Abe invited her to work on a Habitat for Humanity project he was overseeing for an AME Zion church, whose volunteers wore hot pink T-shirts that said "FBI" on the front and "Firm Believer in Christ" on the back. The build site was located in an industrial part of West Charlotte, across the street from a body shop with a spray-painted mural of a man dancing with his legs bent at awkward angles. The words "Dirty South" were painted at the top of the mural. Overhead, they could hear low-flying planes leaving the airport. Mandy and David came to support Karleen and the work she was doing—David by lifting and hammering and Mandy by smiling at Karleen from a folding chair on the edge of the lawn, far enough away so that a stray board or nail could not hurt the baby.

At the first fifteen-minute break, Abe spread out a blanket on the bed of his truck so David and Karleen could sit down.

"We sure do appreciate all you're doing for Karleen," David said. "I'm glad she's got somebody looking out for her."

The truck was parked between a culvert and a highway, and the air smelled like car exhaust and swamp.

"Karleen looks out for herself," Abe said.

David rapped his knuckles against the back window of the cab, where Abe had put a shiny new sticker that read "Driver Carries Only $20 Worth of Ammunition." "Well, you're good at the intimidation anyhow," David said to Abe. "I wouldn't try to mess with you."

She could feel her cheeks burning. David had a way of talking to people that sounded complimentary but wasn't. "The sign isn't just for show," Karleen said. "I've seen him shoot rats on site."

When the time came to stand in a circle, hold hands, and pray, she stood beside Abe. His hand was rough and warm, and she could feel herself inching closer. She couldn't say what she felt, except that she liked standing beside him.

She came to work early on Monday, leaving her house with the street still pitch-dark and the streetlights still glowing, and found Abe in the trailer, checking e-mail.

"Thank you for Saturday," she said. "I never installed floorboards before."

He swiveled his chair around toward her. He wasn't smiling, but his eyes were bright. He told her she was a quick study and could come back the next week to learn about drywall.

"You're nice to help me," she said. "Maybe I could take you to dinner as a thank-you. I have a two-for-one coupon to Mama Ricotta's on Kings."

He turned back to the computer screen, saved the e-mail he'd been writing and minimized the window. The trailer was chilly, and he was wearing a knit cardigan with large oblong buttons, the type of garment somebody would spend months knitting. She pulled a loose thread from the hem of her jeans and put it in her pocket. The back of Abe's neck was mottled with sunburn.

"That doesn't—" she said. "I mean . . ."

He nodded. "Yes," he said. "You name the day."

"Friday," she said. "Friday at six."

That afternoon, she meant to talk to Shanda about Abe and how making friends with him might be a good thing she was doing for herself, but it might also be dangerous. She didn't trust her judgment. The sight of Abe's thin, sun-spotted hands, or the careful way he held a jigsaw, made her want to spend time with him, but the thought of what might happen if the two of them were alone scared her. She had been raised to understand that the worst kind of woman was the one who flirted with a man she didn't want to sleep with, let him do things for her because of his attraction, and she knew that if Abe wanted to sleep with her, she couldn't tell him no.

What she said to Shanda was, "I do not have good sense about men. JT used to send me e-mails saying the only way out was if he killed me, and I still stayed."

Shanda perked up. "You have them?"

"What?" she said. "The e-mails?"

Shanda nodded. Her weave was growing out, and her hair fuzzed at the roots.

"Sure," Karleen said. "He sent e-mails like that all the time."

Shanda's face was sympathetic but also focused on the larger plan. She'd thought of something. "You get me those e-mails," Shanda said, "and we can serve him with new charges within the week. An e-mail like that, an actual death threat, that's rare."

That week, the framer who looked like JT's friend brought a grill, hot dogs, and a battery-operated radio, which was tuned to the local hip-hop station. Avery, who was bouncing his shoulders to the music, pointed to a bucket that was on the ground beside the other roofers. Karleen turned it over and sat down. Her soda was lukewarm and her sandwich was damp with condensation.

"You don't eat meat?" said a light-skinned black guy with freckles on the bridge of his nose.

"I didn't bring any," she said. "I brought a sandwich."

"Hey Mike!" he called. "Get this girl a hot dog."

She looked at her boots.

Mike turned. "We don't have hotdogs for snitches," he said.

The guy with freckles laughed. "Come on," he said. "You should always feed a good-looking woman."

Mike shook his head. "Not this one," he said. "I know who you are, Karleen."

"Drama," Avery said.

Karleen left her sandwich on the overturned bucket and walked over to the grill. Her heart was racing. "Listen, Mike," she said. "JT doesn't need to know where I am." She thought about pulling up her shirt to show him her scar, but she didn't want him looking at her body. "He might be your 'bro' or whatever," she said. "But he's not a good guy."

"You think JT's interested in you?" he said. "He isn't."

She moved closer, so he could see her face. "You aren't going to tell him."

"Drop it," he said. "Nobody cares where you are."

That night she couldn't sleep. David and Mandy were having sex. Mostly, David just breathed loudly, but her sister squealed and shouted, "Keep doing it exactly like that!" and "Baby, I love you so much!"

Mandy had told her that sex in the second trimester was the best she'd ever had. "It's a thing," she said. "It's in the pregnancy books. It's an issue of blood flow."

In the afternoons when David was still at work, Mandy liked to tell her about sex toys and positions. Mandy seemed to want Karleen to understand that being a Christian and being married to the only man you'd ever slept with didn't mean you had to be boring, but Mandy's stories always struck her as sweet. David might tie Mandy up with handcuffs, but Karleen could hear him giggling with her and telling her she was beautiful. Toward the end with JT, sex was only punishment or apology. Often, if she told him he was hurting her, he got excited and hurt her more, and so she lay as still as possible and kept her mouth shut until it was over.

On Friday morning before work, Karleen tried on her wicker high heels and the cotton sundress she'd worn to her high school graduation and stood in front of the full-length mirror in the hallway. It was tighter on her butt and back than it had been before, and now it was too sexy.

"Wow," Mandy said. "You look pretty."

"Did I wake you up?"

Mandy shook her head and leaned against the wall behind her. She was wearing pajamas with yellow moons and stars against a navy background. "You have a date."

Karleen blushed. "No," she said. "Definitely not."

All day, she worried about whether Abe would kiss her. Sweeping up drywall, she found herself imagining that he would try to feel her up on the car ride home, and almost knocked someone off his stilts before she snapped out of it. At shift's end, she lingered with cleanup and then, after they'd put the company tools, goggles, and lumber in the trailer, she followed Abe to his truck.

"Can we meet at the restaurant?"

He opened the passenger's door and got inside. "I'll look forward to it," he said. "Six o'clock, right?"

He started the engine, and the radio came on with a country song about a porch and a girl. He was waiting for her to walk to her car and get it started, and she wondered how her butt looked in her jeans and if her boots made her seem to be strutting, and then she saw a white truck idling on the corner behind a crepe myrtle. She knew before she saw him that JT had found her. She started running. Abe's truck was twenty feet away. Her heart was pounding, and she couldn't think straight.

"Abe," she said. "Help me."

"Huh?"

"There's a white truck on the corner that belongs to my ex. He wants to hurt me."

Abe told her to get inside the passenger's seat and lock the door.

"He's not supposed to come within a hundred feet of me," she said. "He's not supposed to know where I am."

"This is the one you got away from?"

She nodded. "I have scars," she said. "I'll show you." She lifted her shirt.

He kept his eyes in the rearview mirror. "I believe you," he said. "It's okay."

"Just look, please." She pulled up the edge of her bra so he could see the shiny white swirl of skin that ran along her ribs. She wanted him to know.

Abe shook his head. His neck was red, and he was breathing hard. "You're safe now," he said. "He won't hurt you again."

He left the engine running but put the car in park. He reached across her and took a pistol and a box of rounds from the glove compartment.

"What are you going to do?" she said.

"You get down real low," he said. "Crawl down onto the floor if you can fit."

"Abe."

"You're okay," he said.

She pushed the seat back and lowered herself onto the floor mat with her knees up against her chest. In the side mirror, she could see the white truck speeding over the clay toward them. She took out her cell phone and called Shanda, but her cell went to voicemail.

When JT got out of the car, Abe was standing across from him with his pistol cocked.

"Is this a standoff?" JT said. "I'm here to talk to Karleen about a legal matter."

"You aren't talking to her about anything," Abe said. "You need to leave."

"And you are?" JT said. "You are who, exactly?"

She knew JT and how he was. He didn't do well with people telling him what to do. He'd get himself killed before he would listen.

"I'm not leaving," JT said. "Karleen is my wife." Then, calling out, he said, "Karleen? I know I hurt you. I'm sorry, Karleen. Can you come out here? Can we talk?"

"Come on, now," Abe said. "You've done enough to that girl. You leave her be."

She moved her head up a little. JT was wearing a suit and holding a bouquet of roses. He was thinner than usual, and his hair had grown out. He turned in her direction. "I see you," he called out, walking toward her. "You've got to talk to me Karleen," he said. "You can't throw around charges like attempted murder and then hide."

Karleen opened the truck door and let her legs slide out in front of her. They felt loose and numb. She hadn't seen JT since he'd been on top of her, stomping on her, since she'd had to play dead until he left the room. "I'm not hiding," she said, her voice braver than she felt. "I just don't want to see you."

They were in a triangle now, the three of them, nobody more than ten feet from anybody else. In the distance, across the street and behind the trees, the traffic on the highway was whirring past.

"You almost killed me," she said. "My eyes don't move right anymore."

JT shook his head and swallowed hard like he was trying not to choke. His face had a funny expression on it as if he'd suddenly forgotten where he was. "I didn't want you to leave me."

"You hurt me," Karleen said. "You put me in the hospital."

He came toward her, close enough that she could see the sweat on his forehead. "I wasn't the only one," he said. "You know what you did."

Abe held the pistol in the air and fired a warning shot as loud as fireworks. "Stop while you're ahead."

JT kept walking. "You don't know her," he said. JT was in front of her now, with his arms open like he was going to hug or tackle her.

"This is it," Abe said. "Stop moving."

"JT," Karleen said. "Please."

"We're going to talk," he said. "That's what I came for, and I'm not leaving—"

A second shot rang out, and JT crumpled. His hand was pressed against his chest. Karleen stood over him. "Oh my God," she said. "Oh shit. JT."

"He won't die over it," Abe said, his pistol still out in front of him. "I got his shoulder. You want at him?" He gestured to the pistol.

She shook her head but found herself moving closer. JT's eyes were blinking with pain, and he was moaning. Curled up, he looked small. His face was pinched and red, and his jacket was covered in blood.

"So you're fucking this guy?" JT said. "Is that it?"

She meant to kick him once in the ribs so he would know what it felt like to have the wind knocked out of him, but then her boot made contact, and she couldn't stop. Something inside her had snapped, and she wanted to break him.

"I'm not who you came for," she said. "I'm different now."

"Jesus, Karly," he said. "Come on."

His hands were covering his face and his knees pulled into his chest, trying to avoid her blows. He sounded like a child, pleading. She could walk away. He'd broken the terms of his bail and would go to prison. He'd come for her in the first place because he was desperate, because she finally had the evidence to put him in prison. She knew that, but she also knew the bones of the body, the tiny spaces that would hurt forever if you hit the right spot with just enough force.

THE STREET MUSICIAN

Kareem Tayyar

Is playing John Prine's "Angel From Montgomery,"
And for whatever reason,
Maybe because the pier is almost empty this afternoon,
Or that the only girl you ever knew from Alabama is one who
Never loved you back,
It seems like the saddest song you've ever heard.

He seems to feel this way too,
Because he is singing the song so softly that you can't make
Out his voice above the waves,
His guitar like a small boat in the middle of a big storm
    That might not ever make it back to shore.

HOT BATHS

SANDRA KOHLER

*Nearly all the Iliad takes place far from hot baths. Nearly all of
human life, then and now, takes place far from hot baths.*
—Simone Weil, *War and the Iliad.*

In Pakistan, almost three hundred pupils killed
in their classrooms, shot in the head by militants
attacking a school for children of the military.
In Missouri, the unarmed man, robbery suspect,
cut down by a policeman whom the grand jury
refuses to indict. In Brooklyn, two policemen
ambushed and executed by a mentally ill killer
seeking vengeance. In Palestine children recruited
as suicide bombers. Beheadings of journalists by
ISIS terrorists. Genocide in Sri Lanka, Burma, Syria.
In Nepal, protesters burn themselves to death.

This is today's list. In a week, in a month there
will be a different list, as like this one as the Iliad's
formulaic phrases are to each other. Reading the
Iliad, reading newpapers, I think of the acts of
killing in that poem of death, their brutal specificity,

Homer's depiction of how in combat living bodies
are dismembered, each inflicted blow piercing a
different organ, the precise nature of the wound.
No one is spared, nothing. At war's end, Priam
imagines being mutilated by his own dogs, his
gray hair muddied, smeared with blood, privates
exposed, the ugliness of his mortality revealed.

All powerful Zeus, God of the Iliad, is powerless
to change his own son's fate. Agamemnon blames
Zeus for all his mistakes, yet views him as victim
of delusion. Greatest of gods, innocent pawn. God
whom I call on and doubt, do the horrors I recite
prove your non-existence or your indifference?
Does it matter that our lives, even those of the poor,
of children, have grown slowly more bearable over
centuries: fewer dying young, fewer malnourished,
deformed, afflicted? Weil was right; even now
much human life takes place far from hot baths.

DISCIPLES, SOLDIERS AND KINGS

Søren G. Palmer

Naturally, the elevator was broken, so Detective Peters took the stairs, carrying the sneakers in a plastic bag marked "Evidence." Clothes were never fit to return, the shirt ripped away to pull bullets from the stomach or crack open the chest. Jeans caked in blood or sliced down the side for autopsy. But the shoes usually stayed unblemished, save some splatter that could easily be cleaned. Kicks, the kids called them. Currency. Sometimes, if he arrived at a crime scene too late, the kicks would already be gone, the corpse splayed in the street with socked feet.

Shouts rattled down the stairwell, laced with the deep bass of stereo. Cockroaches gathered around a Capri Sun still punctured by a straw. Spray-painted tags designated the building as Gangster Disciple territory: a sloppy, six-pointed star with pitchforks planted on each side of the tip. The wings of a blue heart tried to flutter past a steel door. Three flights up the squeals of rubber soles and laughter crept down the stairs, a raw symphony of youth descending toward Peters until a girl and a boy – eight? Nine? – turned a corner and fired their fingers as guns. Bullets blistered off their lips.

"What up, five-oh?" the boy yelled, still firing, the girl mimicking him two steps above.

Peters feigned being shot in the gut and fell back against the wall, sliding past an upturned crown stuck to the bottom of another pitchfork. "You got me."

"We got five-oh!" The boy slapped the girl a high-five and they sprinted up the stairs, the heels of the boy's high tops flashing red. Their voices wailed like sirens: "Five-oh, five-oh, five-oh!"

As Peters stood, the building's commotion eased into a hush. After two more flights it felt like his lungs were stuffed into tiny boxes and a cough tickled the back of his throat. The kicks in the bag were the latest LeBrons, Nike Zoom Soldier Nine, blue and black with orange trim. Peters had become fascinated with high tops the first time he returned a pair of Air Jordans back in the eighties, and soon after he started roaming Foot Lockers on his lunch hour. Keeping up with trends. Once he'd arrested a Latino Kings regional commander wearing a pair of Golden KB8s, and the kid had been impressed when Peters identified them on sight. Sneaker-speak, the guys in the precinct called it, or laughed about him being the "Shoe Whisperer" as he left with another evidence bag.

She answered the door indignantly and then stepped into the small opening, as if he might try to sneak in. A lanky woman with fists for cheekbones. She wore dark tights, and the silhouettes on her T-shirt faded into the advertisement for a South Side dance studio. He was used to the routine. The anger. The flexible clichés buckling under a last chance to define their child: "He was really a good kid" and "He had a good heart" and "If he'd just stayed away from those monsters." But this woman—her left hand on the door above her head, her toes pointed out and the heel of her front foot scraping the instep of her back—surprised Peters with, "He lasted longer than I thought."

"I'm sorry," Peters said. "I'm sure he was a good kid at heart."

She cocked her jaw, those fists ready to take a few swings. "You are, huh?"

"Well, yeah. Aren't they all?"

"That's some Hallmark hope right there."

Peters raised the bag, cautiously.

"I ain't blind."

"I know, ma'am."

"Good at heart." Her left hand pushed the door open another six inches. She looked to be fighting off sadness, as if it was a bulky jacket she couldn't pull her arms from. The zipper caught and the sleeves awkward. "You know what happens to good at heart around here?"

He ran a hand across his lip. "Yes, ma'am."

"Oh, you know us like that."

"I see what happens."

"So you bring back them shoes."

He kicked at the carpet. His arches ached from the climb and the dress shoes pinched at his toes.

"Those LeBrons got any answers inside them?"

"We're still working the case."

"Can't arrest a place." She bit down on the left side of her lip, and then all her composure seemed to collapse into the small opening on the opposite side of her mouth. "I taught every Saturday to get those."

Peters nodded at her shirt. "Is that where you work?"

"I tore up my knee in ballet, then got pregnant."

"I'm sure he appreciated how hard you worked."

"He was past the age of appreciation." She slid her right hand up the door jam, almost elegantly, then rested her head against it. "But you should've seen him strutting around this apartment like he was royalty. Happiest I've seen him in seventeen years."

The two kids from the stairwell ran past Peters and down the hall, still singing out their warnings, "Five-oh, five-oh, five-oh."

Her gaze drifted down the hall, following the heels of the boy's flashing red sneakers, and then she let her right hand fall from the doorjamb to her stomach. "Will you take them out of the bag? Please?"

Peters nodded, then opened the bag and removed the left shoe – which she snatched from his hand and put to her nose, then closed her eyes and took in a deep breath. The last touch she didn't get or words she couldn't say or warning she forgot to give. Zip up your coat and give me a hug and don't forget that I love you. All of it whittled down to that high top, the tread barely worn.

FOURTH OF JULY ON THE AMERICAN RIVER

Matt Farrell

Another boy
drowned today.
His leg caught under a branch.
The current made quick work of him.
Cottonwood leaves spun free of their stems,
drifted downward and landed
delicately on the water.
There was more silence than noise.

It's always boys the river takes.
Beneath the water-sculpted rocks
is a vast stone room
where they are lined up
like terracotta soldiers
of a great, long-dead emperor.

ALL THE BREATHLESS PEOPLE OF THE SUN

DONELLE DREESE

They sift underneath furniture cushions
passion hunting, gathering lint-caked coins
having fallen from blue jean pockets.

They are sun-lovers who roll in fields
of wild strawberries until their hair turns red
and their eyes are phosphorescent mushrooms.

They are ordinary hermits who swam up
from the bottom of a shivering sea trailing eelgrass
to become all the breathless people of the sun.

They have been sculpted by a cold chisel
that left them eccentric and askew
but brilliant and fearless illuminators.

They are hungry flowers crafting the world.
They drink their water from a cracked cup
and somehow always have enough.

TAKING NOTES

Zlatina G. Sandalska

The Monday after communism collapsed, my best friend Rose and I met on the corner between our two apartment buildings half an hour before our fourth-grade classes began, as always.

It was a wet November morning in Sofia, Bulgaria. The molting tree branches draped over us, heavy with rain drops, like part of some magical archway in a fairy tale.

The gray streets were gray, the wet asphalt darker than usual and covered with patches of red and yellow leaves, like water colors spilling into each other. People hurried to work carrying espressos in thin plastic cups and pastries wrapped in paper. A mother scolded a child who wore a colorful wool hat and dragged his feet, then she stopped him to wipe snot from under his runny nose.

As we walked the two short blocks to school, Rose and I talked about the usual: our two dachshunds. Hers had found a tennis ball in the park and dragged it home, mine peed in the living room; boys—we had crushes on two best friends who flirted with us; homework—I'd let her copy math if she let me copy biology. I hated biology.

When we reached the schoolyard, the porter was already ringing the bell. He was a sturdy old man with thick white hair and glasses, and he paced up and down the courtyard as he waved the heavy, worn brass bell, usually a little late or a little early but generally *around* the time class was supposed to begin or end. (So many times we prayed to the god we weren't supposed to believe in that he'd ring it five minutes early when, during the final moments of class, a teacher decided to call one of us up for oral exams.)

Rose and I hurried into the small building, painted light green with white trimmings, like the house of candy in the Hazel & Gretel tale. A banner celebrating its 125 year anniversary hung above the front entrance.

Each desk in our homeroom sat two pupils, and Rose and I were not allowed to sit together because we talked too much. We had been best friends forever and—of course—there was so much to say, especially during class.

When our fourth-grade home teacher, Comrade Boyanova, entered, she was wearing, as usual, a dark skirt suit, plain like the garbs of a nun. All of us stood up, as we always did.

Rose didn't. She sat, legs crossed, defiantly staring at the woman.

None of us had seen such behavior before. When the teacher walked in, we always stood up. It was a sign of respect, it was the rule and anything else was unimaginable. Until now.

In a small sea of navy uniforms with white collars, we recited in unison, "Good morning, Comrade Boyanova."

Rose said nothing—just slouched in her chair.

As good communist children, or "pioneers," we were supposed to sit upright; slouching and crossing one's legs, especially for a girl, especially in the presence of an older person, especially a teacher, was considered extremely improper and disrespectful.

Ignoring Rose, Comrade Boyanova marched across the room to her desk.

Rose unbuttoned her uniform that looked like a blue lab coat to reveal first a T-shirt and then jeans. Jeans were a sign of Western bourgeois decadence and were therefore banned at school.

Comrade Boyanova carefully placed her purse on her desk. Her straight graying hair was cut in a stringy, controlled bob and her composure was of steel. "You may sit," she calmly said to the rest of us.

She was an ardent communist, taught grammar and was very strict. She had authority that no one in the school had defied before, I was sure. All of our friends' older siblings remembered her well, years after graduating. Cerberus, they called her.

We sat and awaited further instruction.

Then, suddenly, Rose proceeded to pull the hair tie from her smooth ponytail and shook her head so that her long hazel hair splayed out.

The rules about hair were as follows. If you were a boy, it had to be less than two inches short. If you were a girl, short hair like a boy's was encouraged, excessively long was not allowed, and all medium-length had to be tied back. Under no circumstances was hair to be loose.

But that did not stop Rose that day. In the most daring gesture I had ever witnessed, perhaps equivalent to Lenin pointing toward future progress, Rose ran her fingers through her shiny hazel strands, shaking them out as if dispersing devils. It felt like the space-time continuum was being ripped and I was entering a wholly different universe.

"Tie your hair back," Comrade Boyanova said. She clutched the coarse wooden stick she used for pointing on the board like it was a bone and she a hungry dog.

I sat two desks away and smelled Rose's Palmolive shampoo, a further sign of her dissident family. In our Bulgarian pharmacies, one could buy only one of two types of shampoo: calendula, which was bright orange in color, with a picture of the plant on the front, and green apple, the liquid bright green and packaged in a bright green plastic bottle. Rose's parents always had expensive, Western cosmetic products that her father brought from Poland.

"You can't tell me what to do any more," Rose said. She slouched in her chair as the rest of us still stood, in shock, gaping I'm sure. The small defiant smile on her lips perhaps might have angered anyone, not just a widowed old communist teacher who had witnessed the system—to which she dedicated her youth and life—crumble in front of her eyes just days before.

Comrade Boyanova's jaw began to tremble. She raised the wooden stick and slammed it on her desk, the sound like a cannon at Christmas. "This is still my classroom and I will continue to dictate how my students behave," she said. "You will tie your hair."

Comrade Boyanova had always disliked Rose because Rose was sassy and rebellious. Even at that young age, Rose already had certain freedom of movement with her body, a zest for life and a sexiness I think she inherited from her mother, an architect. The two dressed stylishly and pranced in the same way, gazelle-like, swaying their beautiful hips from side to side. Sexiness, too, was frowned upon—of course—as it was another bourgeois vice.

Our teacher disliked Rose also because she came from a "bourgeois" family—her grandfather had been a prominent lawyer and minister of agriculture during the Tsar, an important post as most of Bulgaria's income came from agriculture. When the communists came to power in 1945, they imprisoned him and eventually shot him. Rose's grandmother and her two small children, Rose's father and aunt, were removed from their home and forced to live in the cold, moist basement of an old apartment building outside the city. Perhaps because of this familial history, Rose has always been able to sniff out the communist teachers, i.e., the true believers in the ideology.

Rose was not the best student; she always did her homework but didn't care deeply about learning. She did it because she had to and she'd get in trouble at home if she didn't get good grades. Plus, when the homework was out of the way, she could do more fun things, like watch movies and try on her mother's high heels.

Comrade Boyanova liked me because I was a good student, quiet and obedient, loved school and never caused trouble. She respected my grandparents and all they had done to build communism in Bulgaria. To her, as to many others, it was unbelievable, perhaps even blasphemous, that Rose and I were friends.

That day, while the entire class stood in silence, Comrade

Boyanova promptly sent Rose to the principal's office.

I next saw Rose at the plenary session the principal called at lunch in the schoolyard. As I waited for everyone to gather, a yellow leaf tore itself away from its mother branch and spiraled downward like a graceful Russian ballet dancer, descending on stage from some invisible prop. It made me smile.

Extending behind me was the narrow, cobblestoned street on which Rose and I were born a day apart in the maternal ward of Sofia University. Our mothers had met in the ward but never became friends. To my left, was the steep, one-way street on which large red city buses sped down from the university, three blocks away, to the military academy around the corner, with its pretty, ornamented cast-iron fence and its forest that seemed lush year-round.

Finally, everyone gathered. Then Rose came out and ran to me. We stood next to each other watching the gesticulations of the principal, Mister Misteroff. We were no longer to call him "Comrade Misteroff," he declared, and this new repetition made us laugh too hard. Bald, full of life, red-faced, he stood on the stoops and talked to all of us, little confused happy kids gathered below him. He spoke excitedly but firmly.

"What did he say to you in the office?" I whispered.

"He gave me tea," Rose said. "And said he knew where I was coming from but I still had to respect my teachers." She glanced at him admiringly. He was a bald red-faced jolly man, plump and full of life; he looked like he enjoyed life. He was a flirt and part of Rose's parents' milieu. He was not exactly rule-abiding, did things his own way and hence, we concluded, was a sympathizer to the anti-communist cause.

He seemed happy that day.

We both had a girly crush on him.

I looked up at him. He was saying we no longer needed to bring our textbooks to school or read them, even. The entire school cheered. He talked about responsibility, about a careful transition and that from now we wouldn't use our textbooks—our teachers would lecture and we would take notes.

"Why can't we use the textbooks?" I asked.

"They are propaganda," Rose whispered, leaning forward on her toes to get closer to my ear. "They are written by communists. It's all lies."

I had no awareness of the issues. My grandmother, who had been in the resistance and fought to bring socialism to Bulgaria, employed every bit of communist rhetoric I was already familiar with from school and TV, thus enveloping me further in the mantle of monolithic discourse. According to her, everything was wonderful, the country was in prosperity, and our family was perfect. My grandfather was too busy building communism to spend time with me. My parents avoided any talk of politics, the way American parents avoid any talk relating to sexuality. I think they believed everything was so absurd, there was nothing to discuss; better to read *Winnie the Pooh* and *Alice in Wonderland*—there were universal truths in that, they said. Perhaps, they were simply frightened.

The only hints that there was something bigger lurking in the background came from Rose. Her parents and their friends spoke against the regime at home. Rose was not supposed to hear, let alone tell outsiders like me, but things came out, like when she said that our president, Todor Zhivkov, was a moron. I knew that, of course—whenever he came on TV, my parents sighed and turned off the screen or went to another room—but I was unaware that he was part of a bigger system. I simply thought it was the nature of being a president. It seemed they were all idiots: ours was literally stupid, Ceausescu malicious and a monster, Tito also a monster. They repeated empty phrases and senseless lies in long speeches at communist congresses and holidays like May Day and New Year's. What was new?

The other hint was Rose's grandmother, who had developed a severe form of thrombosis as a result of living in the cold, moist basement. The veins on her legs had expanded so much, her legs were fat like baobab trees. She could barely move. Not able to lift her feet, she dragged her feet forward a few centimeters at a time. She used a cane, sometimes two. It took her an entire hour to cross Rose's small living room, where Rose and I played in the afternoons after school. But the old lady had an authority and Rose and I were both scared of her regal manner. We zoomed by her like she was a massive planet, never speaking to her, both drawn and repelled by her handicap.

When my own grandmother fussed around with presentation or was excruciatingly concerned with how things looked in front of "the community," my father accused her of being "bourgeois," the most severe of offenses. The bouregoisification of the communist middle class had taken place in the 1960s, when quality of life was relatively good and families acquired domestic comforts such as fridges and laundry machines. But my grandmother was more of a nouveau riche than an actual bourgeois of the kind Marx talks about. She came from peasant stock. The communist government, in an attempt to reverse the power structure, had put her (and others like her) on top, as a result of which my grandmother had become part of the ruling class. Even at the time, I knew there was something not quite right: she had substantial responsibilities in prominent women's committees, acted uppity, yet when she gave me birthday cards, she misspelled simple words like "happiness" and "success" and used bad grammar. Her handwriting was crude and circular like that of an orphaned gypsy.

Rose's grandmother, on the other hand, was a real bourgeois, the kind one saw in French films. Her handwriting was even and graceful—I saw it on book inscriptions and cards she gifted Rose for holidays. She came from a long line of prominent lawyers and businessmen. She owned actual bourgeois things, like antique jewelry passed on for generations. She owned oil portraits of herself with pearls and perfectly manicured blond waves, of her husband in his minister's office and of Rose's father and aunt as children in frills and curls.

At some point, the authorities must have rehabilitated her, or at least decided there was little reason to abuse an apolitical woman and her two small children. Perhaps family friends intervened on her behalf. When he got a bit older, Rose's father was even allowed to study in Poland, which was practically "The West" for us, and from there he later brought her "Western" things like "jeans," although these were not Levi's but Polish imitations of the American brand. Still, they were something.

In the weeks after the regime collapsed, changes began to take place. We no longer had to wear uniforms or take Russian class, unless we wanted to. Nobody wanted to. Rose dropped

it instantly—she had always despised everything Russian. I
tried for a few more weeks—I didn't want to disappoint my
Russophile grandparents. But it was a ridiculous venture: to
make a sentence, you had to learn five declensions for three
genders and change the ending of each word depending on
its function in a sentence. I stopped going. My parents didn't
care—they had never put in much effort into learning the
language either. The true idealist, my father probably believed
one didn't need grammar but only heart and humanity
to communicate with people from different cultures—his
Hungarian friends visited in summers, yet they didn't speak
each others' languages. Plus, my parents did not like to force
us into anything or trample our freedoms. My grandmother
pouted for a few days but got over it fairly quickly.

Mister Misteroff took over our history class. I suppose he
didn't want the older communist teachers to keep filling our
minds with the only things they knew: ideology and propaganda.
Perhaps the order came from above. But I liked listening to his
lectures. He walked up and down the classroom, and spit flew
in all direction as he gestured and lectured, as if for the first
time—and it probably was his first time, in a way. His eyes
popped out when he mock-threatened us as we passed notes
to each other; it made us laugh so hard. He was effervescent,
passionate, a tease, and he cared. I liked taking notes in his class
because it made me feel like an adult, like we were at university,
and I couldn't wait to go there.

In the following months, an '80s explosion finally arrived
at our small country at the end of Europe. The Scorpions
blasted from every café and apartment window. Young people

wore torn jeans and attached chains from their keyholes to their back pockets; many of the older boys put on eyeliner in attempts to look like Robert Smith; haircuts became more disheveled and protrudingly pronounced. Then people began to lose their jobs, shops had not even bread, no one was paid for months, whole industries went on strikes, and, in order to buy groceries, one had to have state paperwork for the rations and wait in line for hours.

But in my clueless version of the universe, life went on as before—I went to school, did my homework, fought and made up with my brother, took my dog to the park, hung out with Rose and went to lunch at my grandparents' every day. I ignored the fact that my grandfather had to spend most of the morning waiting in lines to procure cheese and bribe the sales clerks for a few slices of sandwich meat, and that my grandmother seemed almost paralyzed about the uncertainty of having food for our next meal, and that my parents were present even less.

Then one frosty sunny spring day, the week before our country was to celebrate Easter for the first time in half a century, Rose and I cut class and went to my apartment. We smoked a cigarette on the terrace as we looked across the courtyard onto the school's yard and waited for the porter to ring the bell for the end of the "long break."

He did and things got quiet. The snow had melted recently and water slowly dripped from the wet trees.

No one was home, the neighbors were at work, all of our friends at school. There was no TV during the day. We had no money or guts to go to a local café where we'd be asked why we weren't in class, or to the park, where some pensioner lady baby-sitting her little grandchild would recognize us and ask us why we weren't at school, then report to our grandparents. Then there was nothing to do.

So I said, "Let's go look through my parents' bookshelf." My father had been reading Kurt Vonnegut's *Slaughterhouse-Five* and it sounded funny. Perhaps looking for it would keep us entertained.

My parents didn't like me to enter their bedroom when they weren't present. It was their intimate space, something hard to come by in a controlling regime such as ours had been, where everything was monitored and privacy was denounced. I knew I would be breaking the rules and disrespecting my parents if I went in with Rose. But I also wanted to please Rose, who always had fun things for us to do in her place, like watch bootlegged, illegally-dubbed American romantic comedies on her VCR, like *Pretty Woman* and *Romancing the Stone* and *Uncle Vinnie* and *Indiana Jones,* or try on her mother's high heel shoes or make-up or perfume. In our apartment, there was not even a working record player or radio. We had an old broken stereo system my father had bought as a student and that I had never seen work. My mother owned no perfume, no high heels, and no make-up of any kind.

When we entered my parents' bedroom, it was dark inside. We were on the fifth floor but the linden trees outside were so large and expansive, their branches stretched against the glass. The way the sun fell in the afternoons behind the buildings made it seem even darker. The floor-to-ceiling bookcase spread across the entire wall across the bed.

As we browsed through books by the Strugatskii brothers, Mark Twain, Carl Sagan, Woody Allen, and various sci-fi and humor in Russian and English, Rose saw a miniature booklet on one of the shelves.

She took it in hand and examined it. Each stamp-sized page had a red rose and the letters "BSP" drawn in red. Bulgarian Socialist Party—I knew that. The communist party renamed itself "Socialist Party" practically the day after the collapse. "Two levs," it said at the top of each page; not very much money at all—probably good for a double-espresso and an open-faced grilled cheese sandwich called "princess."

"So it's true," Rose said. "Your parents really believe in this crap?" She looked disappointed, even angry.

Rose loved my parents. Her own father was old-school and authoritative. He always wore serious clothes and had serious discussions with his friends who also wore serious clothes. These dinners lasted for hours. Rose and her sister were never invited, yet they couldn't leave the house and had to show propriety by being there somewhere, hidden. I had stopped by their apartment on several such occasions and her sweet mother quietly shooed me out so Rose wouldn't get in trouble. Rose and her sister had strict curfews, had to attend sit-down family meals, were often grounded, and lied about their grades to avoid getting in trouble. All three women—Rose, her sister and mom—were afraid of her father. The grandmother was not, because he deferred to her.

My parents were fun, especially my father. He sported bell-bottoms and the only time I saw him with a tie, it was made of bright red leather. My mother wore a cerulean winter coat with a yellow scarf (a testament to her resourcefulness and creativity since shops didn't sell anything of the kind); she knitted colorful sweaters and wove bright leather strands through them. My father indulged us and played with us and never kicked us out when his friends came over. My brother and I liked being around them and the jocular atmosphere they created, though of course we couldn't understand their jokes. We lived with no rules, no discipline or disciplining. We could watch anything on TV and read any book we wanted. We could say bad words and whatever was on our minds even in front of our grandparents, the serious communists. We knew they were softies and didn't have the heart to ground us or get mad at us. My father instilled in us the importance of dignity, privacy, self-respect—or tried to anyhow. If anyone wanted to come into our rooms, they had to knock—the total opposite of Rose's household. We were respected, our opinions listened to. It's not that my family was perfect—far from it—but I think that's what Rose saw.

I think what she loved the most was our Sunday trips, when we all piled up in our yellow Trabi, an old East German car with a two-stroke engine made of Duroplast now found only in museums about life behind the Iron Curtain, and drove to a restaurant to eat sundaes. Rose was always invited, with her dog. When we finished, we let our two dachshunds—hers and ours—lick the cups from the ice cream.

I knew Rose's parents (perhaps like Comrade Boyanova) were displeased that she spent so much time with my family, probably because of the difference in political ideology. She often got in trouble and had to lie about where she'd been. On

Sundays, she told her parents she went to walk the dog, when she actually came on drives and ate decadent ice cream desserts with us. I was sure Rose defended my parents in front of hers, said they owned Beatles records and Western books, just as hers did.

That day, when Rose found the donation booklet, she was truly upset.

"I don't know what this is," I said. I really didn't.

"They donated money to the socialists. That's what it means," she said and threw the booklet back on the shelf as if it were a disgusting handkerchief soaked in snot.

After that day, something changed. Rose started putting buttons and safety pins on her jacket, trying to look like Madonna. She wore torn jeans and huge silver loop earrings. Perhaps she hoped that the new political system would change her private universe, that things would be different, that her home-situation would improve.

I started to observe things and try to understand, to take my own life notes, as it were. At our family gatherings, on Sundays, birthdays and holidays, when we went to my grandparents', the adults fought about politics. My father did not agree with my grandfather, a hardened communist, who truly believed Stalin was a great man. At the same time, he violently disagreed with his sister, who had lived in Libya, made good money there, was an Anglophile and probably, a "capitalist." My father had never joined any organizations.

I could tell my parents believed in many of the communist values. Things like compassion, community, and honesty meant a lot to them. They adopted homeless dogs and gave away the little money they had. Our apartment was a constant stampede of their friends, who stopped by for help, a chat, food, or support. My father admired America for its stated ideals of self-expression, self-realization, and individualism. At the same time, he read Marx as a philosopher and was proud of the idealism of his parents, their hard work, and the facts that they risked their lives to join the resistance to fight the Nazis, that they supported ethnic minorities in our country, including the Jews, the Bulgarian Turks, and the Roma.

I also learned that my parents had helped several close friends defect—drove them to the border, gave them money, and covered for them in front of the authorities—and had themselves considered moving to Zimbabwe in the early eighties.

I am sure my parents were glad the regime collapsed but they probably didn't want it to become completely erased, either. The renaming of the Bulgarian party from "communist" to "socialist" must have given them hope. "Socialist" sounded softer, more humanist, like Sweden, and Sweden was a perfect nation, according to all accounts.

I started to pay attention to the news as well. I wanted to figure it out and take a side, although I am not sure I ever did. The newly arrived "democrats" seemed vulgar. Their leaders spoke Bulgarian incorrectly—they ate the ends of words and, like my grandmother, used bad grammar. Some of them were monarchists and I knew I never wanted a king in my country again—entitlement by birth made even less sense than an idiot president. The "democrats" had no dignity; they acted like lapdogs to every Westerner who showed interest in our country.

They wanted to punish people, destroy the communist statues, and thus reverse the past my grandparents had built.

What I learned was that reality was complicated. Dissenting conservatives, authoritarian liberals—none of it made sense, but it did because it all involved humans. I had to navigate to my own truth somehow. Perhaps it would take a lifetime.

Comrade Boyanova retired (or was retired) and we received a new shipment of young teachers straight out of university, educated during perestroika. And they were awesome.

The new English teacher's black leather miniskirt and green eyes bewitched us all. But it wasn't just that. Instead of learning only grammatical rules in her class, we had actual conversations in English and imagined we lived in rainy UK, and reenacted funny scenes of British life. The two boys Rose and I liked didn't want to play with us any more because they just wanted to study English.

The new art teacher had huge protruding eyebrows and looked like an owl. But he encouraged us to paint nature and fruits the way we saw them. We no longer drew the neo-classical architecture of the mausoleum of Georgy Dimitrov, the Bulgarian Lenin, or the building of the president in black and white. We used color and imagination, and there was nothing better than that.

Ms. Marinova, the new history teacher, was a redhead with long hair in a high ponytail. She wore bright green skirt suits and told us fascinating stories about the ancients and the first houses built on stilts above water. Once, I was so frustrated by the conversion of Roman numerals for the century into years, I started to cry in class. Ms. Marinova squatted down next to my desk and gently, discreetly explained to me how to convert year 1787 to a century while everyone else did an assignment.

Our new home teacher, Ms. Bozhkova, a beautiful blond woman, deeply cared about each of us. She had intense dark blue eyes, was always elegant in her high heels, and took us on fun trips to museums and historical sites. In spring, during writing class we went to the park when the lilac bushes were blooming. Our assignment was to journal about them—or anything we wanted. Once, I turned in an essay from the point of view of a man's tie; it showed how oppressive it was to wear one. Ms. Bozhkova gave me an A. Her comment said, "Indeed, how many things we are enslaved by!"

And through all this, Rose and I stayed best friends.

BIRTHNIGHT

Joe Cottonwood

I was born on August 19, 1947.
I have proof: a hospital bill
handwritten in script, blue ink,
from Sibley Hospital in Washington DC
for one childbirth, $48 stamped PAID.
My mom probably picked up the tab.
Dad was careless with pennies and sperm.

On that swampy-hot summer evening
Dad must have driven us home in that
wood-sided Willys, no seat belts, bouncing
beside the Potomac River so broad and so quiet,
the B&O railroad tracks, the coal trains
like black snakes, the C&O canal
in moonlight, the sycamores
heavy with leaves.

In the crumbling brick house
of too few rooms I would sleep
in a closet, for fourteen years my bedroom
was a closet and yet I would grow,
I would leave pennies on the tracks,

swim the river, walk every step of the canal
all the way to West Virginia with a girl
who would hold my hand and kiss my lips
and lie with me among sycamores,
with her I would grow to be a man, a father,
grandfather of wonders who kayak many a river,
who climb many a sycamore,
setting many a penny
on many a track.

SHAVER

E. Laura Golberg

I watch my father wet the brush,
push it into the soap,
bristles twirling, splaying
to get the full coat of lather.
He applies brush to face in circular
motions, leaving thick foam.
More soap. Pulling top lip taut
over teeth, he covers it with white.

He draws the razor through suds
leaving bare skin
like a train bed through snow,
till his face is clear,
stipple of beard gone.

Somewhere under the soap,
is the man whom shaving
doesn't reveal, though I watch
and watch and watch again.

PICKUP BALL IN THE PARKING LOT OF HEAVENLY DELIGHTS

Robert P. Kaye

Late spring, 1992

Dave stepped into the fenced alcove by the dumpster and retrieved Louis from his hiding place. He took a chop with the bat, placing an imaginary shot between first and second, remembering high school when he could put the ball anywhere he wanted.

Late night air filled his lungs with the chill of impending dew. A small brown bat sliced through a cloud of insects in the pool of light surrounding the big pole erected in the center of the parking lot—a small bat, hunting long after its brethren had retired for the evening.

He would so miss this.

The soundproofed door to the strip club opened on the chorus of "Gimme Shelter," rape and murder just a shot away, just a shot away. Which meant either Destiny or Mercedes worked the pole. They bickered over the exclusive rights to the song and its power to extract bills from the PLs in the slobber row.

PLs. Pathetic Losers. The term still made him squirm a little.

Promise slipped out the door in her kimono robe and

mules, clopping down the side of the building. He imagined they'd spent the night together and she was coming out into the kitchen to make pancakes. Funny how most of his fantasies had to do with what might be called domestic bliss. They'd never even had sex. Which turned out to be fortunate, given the circumstances.

"Any Romeos waiting to climb the trellis?" she said.

"Gimme a sec." Dave had forgotten why he'd come out in the first place— to recon the lot for the guys who felt they were entitled to more than the chapped dicks they got from the lap dances. Most bouncers bitched about the hassle of escorting the ladies to their cars. He counted it a fringe benefit.

"You okay?"

He could tell she was asking because he'd been sick. The pneumonia that put him in the hospital was an opportunistic infection, the doc said. One of many he'd get with his T-cells on extended vacation. He might die of chickenpox or a bad cold. That bug that lives in kitty litter might have already taken up residence in his brain, turning it to Swiss cheese. The brochures he found hard to read provided further confirmation that no cure existed for AIDS. No sense waiting around to blow out the candles at the end of the pity party. "Yeah, I feel great tonight."

"We need to get Lolita the hell out of here before she starts a riot," Promise said. "I'm back with her in five. All cool out here?"

"Yeah," Dave said. "We're good."

He watched Promise's rockin ass as she walked back to the door, the silk kimono more alluring than any G-string or filmy panties. Nothing ruined naked like working in a skin shop.

He hid Louis again, so as to not to spoil the surprise, and turned to inventory the usual spots where the lurkers lingered. Three figures clustered behind the laurel hedge between the parking lot and the gas station, a spot also favored as an outdoor toilet. Dave recognized the three ATMs Lolita'd been making withdrawals from all night while talking non-stop stripper shit. *Oh, my boyfriend got me addicted to coke, ripped me off and gave me a black eye and now I have no money and a hole in my heart. You have a big dick.* All true. Except the part about the big dick.

He watched the small brown bat make another pass through the bugs. "Chew your food," he said. "Don't get fat and slow." He didn't feel sick. Not tonight.

The heavy padded door opened again. Promise dragged Lolita by the arm half out the door, where she stuck, hanging off the jamb, talking to Spike, the other bouncer, whose real name was George. Inside Jimi played "Foxy Lady," meaning Treasure boggled gravity with her bolt-on 44s, moving in elliptical synchronization with the guitar licks, hypnotizing the customers into parting with larger bills. Strip clubs remained the last refuge of classic rock and soul, the late shift cranking up the oldies to wring a little more out of the older guys too lonely to go home with their cash, nostalgia the best anesthetic for a walletectomy. Dave loved that music too.

"We've gotta split, goddamn it." Promise jerked Lolita free of the door. "Dave's waiting." Promise wore a jean jacket, hair pulled back into a ponytail. A sensible bra confined the considerable rack underneath the flannel shirt. Mall mom jeans concealed the C-section scar she hid with makeup when working. Experienced sexy was still the best sexy.

Promise dragged Lolita down the length of the building. Dave stepped out to meet them, offering his arm.

"Hey, big guy, you might need this." She passed the Louisville Slugger across his back to keep it hidden. Their fingertips brushed as he took the bat, sending a little thrill up his arm. He couldn't help himself.

"Wait a sec, I forgot something." Lolita started back toward the door, the staccato of her heels bouncing off the stucco.

"No you don't, honey." Promise grabbed her wrist, almost jerking her off her heels. "Time to go night-night."

Lolita staggered back around in her full-length raincoat and big dark sunglasses, a disguise rendered worthless by peroxide Marilyn hair flaring in mercury vapor lights. A canvas book bag swung from her elbow with the word READ and a bug-eyed picture of somebody named Virginia Woolf, probably a sci-fi/fantasy writer with a name like that. Lolita was supposedly gathering material for a novel and paying for some artsy master's degree with stripper money. Dave wondered if he'd have a part in the book. It would be cool to be immemorialized like that.

They set out across the blacktop, three abreast. Dave always liked that word, "abreast." It reminded him of high school, when you could laugh at shit like that, unaware of disappointments to come. Long before he got the athletic scholarship. Before he'd majored in partying and flunked out. God, he'd loved college while it lasted.

"So all three of them stuck around?" Promise looked tired

and short on patience.

"Yep." Dave studied the guys in the bushes, who probably thought they were invisible, not realizing the gas station lights silhouetted them like shadow puppets. He wondered how soon she'd quit this life and get a job as a counter clerk at some neighborhood hardware store, all the guys working overtime on crushes.

"Hey, I just wanna talk to these jerks a sec." Lolita bolted to the side, pulling Team Stripper off course, but failing to break Promise's grip.

That kind of behavior had its charm. Like Stasia not taking off her heels at first even in the sack to keep the needle marks between her toes invisible. Sharing those needles had to be why the damn test came back positive. Or the unprotected sex. Stasia didn't work at Heavenly Delights anymore. Another flying thing escaped into the night.

Lolita jerked free, stumblerunning toward the bushes.

"Fuck." Promise ran her down in a few steps, hauling her back. "Work with me, honey. I gotta get my little girl ready for school in like three hours."

He knew two true things about her. One, that she had a daughter, whose name she told no one at the club. Two, that Promise was her real name, her mother having promised she wouldn't get another abortion.

"I just need to say a few words to these guys about subjugation," Lolita said.

Dave didn't know what that meant, but Lolita had meltdown crying fits twice the previous week and broke a mirror in the dressing room, then refused to come out for her set at the pole.

For which Leo kept her club fee and ejected her, yelling perk up or pack up, because sad was bad. For business. Tonight was her first night back. She'd returned as a stripper dynamo.

Promise pulled Lolita close. "Where's your car, honey?"

"Back in the corner," Lolita said. "To make room for the whales, like Leo says."

"Leo's an idiot," Dave said. All the whales went up the street to the club with the VIP room where the pro basketball players sometimes partied. He offered Lolita his arm and she took it. They sandwiched her between them, moving in a cloud of powder and sweat sweet as fresh cut honeydew, the baseball bat like a collective tail. Maybe if Promise had been a cheerleader when he was sacking quarterbacks and hitting homers they would have gotten married and both worked at that hardware store.

"You get better tips when you're ovulating," Lolita said. "I have a graph that proves it."

"Everybody knows that," Promise said.

"It's not like it isn't scientifically proven that women are smarter than men." Lolita called toward the bushes. "Is that why you pathetic losers always have to resort to VIOLENCE?"

They'd almost reached her beater Buick when the PLs emerged into the light, coming across the corner to cut them off from retreat.

Team Stripper, backs to the car, turned to face Team Stupid. The biggest guy walked the point, a curly haired Pillsbury Doughboy a half pace back. The skinny rat face guy hung a few steps back. The one to worry about.

"Get her keys," Dave said.

"On it." Promise stuck both hands in the book bag and rummaged.

Lolita removed her dark glasses, the shiner like a purple dent in an otherwise perfect face now visible beneath the smeared makeup in the harsh light. The raincoat fell open on her camisole and low slung jeans, showing three inches of belly. This stopped the three men cold. She had that effect on guys.

"Girl, where are your damned keys?" Promise said.

"Hey, Lolita," said the biggest of the three, bowl-cut hair making him look like a puffed up John Denver, six-three, two-ten with actual biceps. "You made us some promises."

Dave flashed on the doc at the clinic who came out to give him the results of the blood test. He had that same strawberry blonde hair, but a way better cut and a stud earring. "You know this isn't necessarily a death sentence, right? There's a new drug cocktail that suppresses the virus. It's not like the 80's. You can lead an almost normal life if you're careful."

Suppress, not cure. The thought of dependence on non-recreational drugs made him sick. Dave had always had trouble swallowing pills. "Almost normal" sounded like hell.

"I never promised anything," Lolita said.

"You kinda did." Pillsbury's voice wobbled.

Rat Face remained silent, too calm to be inexperienced.

"Those were word pictures to enhance your enjoyment," Lolita said. "All part of the service. I never promised you shit. Check with my lawyer." She jerked her head toward Dave.

He had sympathy for PLs in general, knowing better than anyone how naked flesh obliterated good judgment. Hadn't any of them noticed Lolita pinballing between the others all evening, juicing them like oranges? Wasn't everyone a PL at the end of the night?

"I asked if you did takeout," Pillsbury said. "You said to meet you in the parking lot after your shift. That sounded like a promise."

"Same here," John Denver said.

Rat Face nodded.

Promise rolled her eyes.

"That's subject to interpretation," Lolita said. "I never said what would *happen* in the parking lot. Right, Dave?"

Dave smiled, the bat still hidden behind his leg. The drug cocktail was ridiculously expensive, month after month, year after year. You had to commit to clinical trials. Show stability. Not one of Dave's strong suits.

"Look, guys," Promise said. "This is not worth going to jail. Or the hospital."

"Knock their fucking heads off, Dave," Lolita screamed, ripping the book bag away from Promise still rummaging for keys. She lunged, swinging the bag. Pillsbury and John Denver danced back, nimble for big guys. Rat Face smirked. Dave hated that smirk.

"Hey, hey, hey." Promise hauled Lolita back by a handful of raincoat and locked an arm around her neck, wrenching the bag away and dumping it out on the blacktop. An overstuffed makeup bag, a thick paperback book, a pint of whiskey, a pill bottle that didn't contain pills and a lot of pens. Fortunately, no big wad of cash.

"Got em." Dave heard the jingle of the keys and felt glad.

"Give the girl a break," Promise said. "She's been through some shit."

"No!" Lolita corkscrewed free. "I don't want your fucking sympathy. I want Dave to fuck them up. And I wanna watch."

There it was. She'd set the whole thing up. Not that it mattered. "Relax, everybody," Dave said. "This doesn't have to end horrible."

Lolita attempted another lunge, but Promise smothered her in a bear hug from behind, hauling her kicking to the car. Team Stupid surged forward and Dave cocked the bat for a double. They fell back. "Easy, guys," Dave said.

Lolita began to whimper. Andy, the object of her affections, was a pudgy guy with a lot of dark hair, a little like Pillsbury. Not someone you'd pick out as a coke dealer. Dave felt for the familiar chip in the heel of the bat with his thumb. It felt normal.

"We all agreed you can keep the money for the lap dances," John Denver said. "You earned that. But I want my tips back. Or my money's worth."

Rat Face snickered, and Dave guessed he wasn't there for money or sex. He hated that guy.

Time for The Speech. "Look, guys. There's no refunds at strip clubs. Here the customer is not always right. You can choose to remember this night fondly as a good time and maybe a lesson learned. If you step up, I will break your bones and you will hate yourselves for being Pathetic Losers even worse than you do now. Trust me on this guys."

For a moment, strippers and Romeos alike seemed to consider his wisdom. Then Rat Face edged further to Dave's flank.

Nobody could say he hadn't offered a fair shake. He took a step forward and punked Louis's business end against the pavement to herd Rat Face back to the center. The solid chip echoed off the side of the building. Echolocation. Batter up. "Get her out of here."

"I'm trying," Promise said.

He heard keys in a lock and the scuffle of Lolita stuffed inside. Saw Promise's hand scoop up the makeup bag and the book and the pill bottle, leaving a heap of change and pens and a little package of tissues. And the pint of bourbon, no doubt for him when this was over.

"Guys, there's nothing left but downside here," Dave slapped the fat end of the bat into his hand. "Get in your cars and drive away and never come back or we play a game of pickup ball. As in, when this is over, you pick up your teeth and your balls."

He smiled, because that's what the line required, but the heavy dew of sadness overcame him. Sad he'd never get a chance to use that line again. Or feel the smack of the fat end of the bat against his palm to punctuate the point. He imagined this as The Big Game, bottom of the ninth, one down, one man on, two outs. All up to him.

He wished Promise worked in a hardware store and he'd taken up his uncle's offer to apprenticed as a plumber. He'd stop by the store for parts.

Rat Face edged deeper into peripheral vision. Dave checked the door of the club and the light pole erected in the center of the lot. The little bat seemed to have retired for the evening.

"Break their fucking heads, Dave," Lolita yelled from the car window as the engine sputtered to life and the transmission thunked into drive.

Pillsbury sprinted for his car on the other side of the lot—a Mercedes no less. Dave felt a bit of a letdown, but then he heard the knife blade lock. He jumped sideways and swung hard at Rat Face's arm, but missed. Rat Face grinned. He fucking grinned.

The car shifted and began to move. He had mixed emotions about the imminent departure of his cheering section, but Rat Face skipped across to his other side, knife held low.

Any second one of them would barrel in. Dave knew Team Stupid's playbook backwards and forwards, having starred on that squad for years. He wondered if it wouldn't be better to have his .38 with him now instead of stowed under the seat for later when he would drive to the top of the hill overlooking the high school stadium and watch the sun come up, highlighting the blurred lines. It wasn't his high school, but it was close enough.

The Buick exited the lot onto the empty arterial with a roar and a bang and Dave thought, shit, one of them has a gun, but Rat Face and John Denver looked equally startled. The Buick belched blue smoke, bald tires squealing, almost colliding with the Mercedes.

Batter up.

SWITCH-BLADE NAMES

ALEX ANDREW HUGHES

They're the unseen writers, ghosts gliding
aboard trains and subways in the evening. The rats
and scattered riffraff blink and cover their ears,
observing the scribes chiseling their humble
epitaphs: three letters to say someone once
lived here, lost in reality's gears. Three letters
to say the dust of the earth is alive. The plastic
seat-back supports the testimony of dozens,
hundreds—so many letters, so many lives, sliced
under cover of night with a blunted knife—
the script is chipped, sharp and angular,
like a child scratching with a ham-fist. Nothing
connects or flows, but comes up short, juts
into superfluity with jagged brutality.
They make to carve their existence with
cracked and bruised hands, proclaiming—no—
pleading—no—needing their letters to matter,
like an *MDS* is somehow better, more worthy
of remembering than an *LDR* or an *ARB*.
And the deepest, largest, most central letters
seem carved with a dominance that fears
obscurity—with a hand that trembles,

sensing the edge. Some day there will be
nothing left, when ten thousand men
and women have left their mark. The plastic
block of hope will be chipped beyond repair,
cracks will spread through their last-ditch dream,
and this monument will be discarded as trash.
Of course they didn't consider this fatal error.
Or maybe they did, but had a premonition
someone would come along looking for
inspiration, using the pen as a switch-blade.

SPARE CHANGE

RICHARD PEABODY

all-purpose
sorcery

ground pepper
magic

scarlet silk
maladies

snickers bars
in sardine cans

paper anvils
lipstick windows

a tryst
a task

a damask

a bottle
full of bullets

HOWARD'S END

Mary Taugher

When Elaine comes home from birding, she finds Howard in the den in his La-Z-Boy chair. The remote control, like a beloved pet, rests in his lap. Eyes closed, he looks like he's napping. He could be napping or he could be thinking, worrying perhaps about his next doctor's appointment. But Elaine knows right away he's not. Howard is dead. A twitch of panic judders down her spine as she forces herself to check Howard's pulse, his hand stiff and cold.

Her panic quickly dissolves into a peculiar lassitude, and Elaine sits down on the desk chair across from her dead husband. His face has taken on the waxy color and droopy texture of a fallen magnolia blossom. His feet lie on the recliner's built-in footrest, his head tilted back with his mouth open, his palms upturned in a gesture that reminds Elaine of a priest's blessing, an absurd thought because Howard hasn't stepped inside a place of worship since his daughter married twenty-six years ago, not even for funerals, of which there have been plenty these past few years in Sun City Village.

Elaine knows she should call someone, 911, her neighbor Rene, or her son Robert who lives nearby. Her nature is to do the correct thing, always, and she's heard stories here in the retirement community about suspicious sheriff's detectives interrogating husbands and wives whose spouses died unexpectedly at home. But a tinge of rebellion fizzes inside Elaine. There's no hurry, she reasons, no bringing Howard back.

The den is dark and cold because Howard always closes the shutters against the insistent sun. Elaine gets up to open them.

Two talking heads on the television squawk and finger-wag, bickering about the upcoming election between the idiot carnival barker and HRC, who reminds Elaine of Ruth Zimmer back in Michigan, a bossy scold. Elaine has the sense that this same footage loops every time she steps in the den. The volume is cranked up so loud that if the neighbors were younger and could hear better, they'd call to complain.

Gingerly she removes the remote control from Howard's lap and snaps off the television. What a relief. She won't have to listen to cable news anymore, or argue with Howard about her decision to not vote. Howard, a retired public relations executive who excelled in public speaking, liked to show off his debating skills and often started a political discussion for the fun of it, always ripping Elaine's reasoning to shreds.

With her binoculars around her neck, Elaine leans over Howard and puts the remote control back in his lap. Where it belongs. Her lack of indecision over this action startles her. It's only as it should be, she tells herself.

Howard had spent far more time these past few years watching the news, the History Channel and old detective shows than he had talking with her. Even then all he did was tut and fuss about the aches and stabbing pains for which none of his doctors could find a reason. When he wasn't worrying about his health, he was complaining about the damn adolescent doctors who were more concerned about their marathons and tech investments than getting to the bottom of what ailed him.

Poor Howard had been right. She thinks of the book she'd recently bought but had chickened out of giving him. *Hypochondria: Woeful Imaginings.* Thank god she'd stashed it the front hall closet behind the remnants of their younger lives, tennis rackets, hiking boots, the lumpy ceramic vases she'd made in the pottery class, the heaps of black-and-white photos from Howard's short romance with photography.

The phone on the desk rings, and she sits down to pick it up. It's her sister Marilyn whose biorhythms have been reversed since early adulthood. Marilyn never rises before two p.m. and it's only noon.

"How are you?" Marilyn asks without waiting for a reply. "I can't remember what time the symphony is tonight."

Elaine can't seem to form words. Perhaps she is in shock. But Marilyn shouldn't be the one to hear the news of Howard's death first. Marilyn, selfish Marilyn, who never got along with Howard. Elaine doesn't bother to keep the annoyance out of her voice. "What are you doing up before lunch?"

"What—"

"Oh never mind," Elaine says. "I'm not going. Give my ticket to someone else. You'll have to find your own ride."

"Someone woke up on –"

"I'm busy," Elaine interrupts. "I'll call you tomorrow."

Marilyn, her younger, prettier thrice-divorced sister, is disturbing the fuzzy feeling that's overcome Elaine. Strange, it's almost relaxing. A horrid thought. Her husband is dead.

Before Elaine hangs up on Marilyn a bizarre idea flits through her mind: Marilyn has a medical marijuana license for her glaucoma and keeps a supply of pot brownies in her freezer. She claims that pot has the added effect of soothing her arthritis and calming her nerves. The next few days and weeks will be tough, full of decisions and relatives, Howard's in particular, she doesn't want to see.

"Elaine, you sound frazzled," Marilyn says. Her laidback voice is laced with the dismissiveness she typically accords Elaine. "Not yourself. Maybe you should get out, away from Howard, and go bird watch or take a walk or –"

"Actually I'm not feeling all that well," Elaine says. "I hurt my back, and don't fall off the side of your bed, but I'm thinking I could use a few of your brownies."

Marilyn gasps with exaggerated surprise. Before her sister can say another word, Elaine asks her to deliver the brownies as soon as possible. Her voice infused with amusement, Marilyn wonders what Howard will think of such unorthodox medication. Elaine tells her not to worry. And when Marilyn protests that she needs to put on makeup and run a few errands, Elaine insists that Marilyn come by as soon as possible, that she wouldn't ask if the pain weren't so bad. She cannot believe her sister agrees without another word.

Elaine stands up from the desk to leave the den, but her feet seem rooted to the floor. She glances at Howard and a prickly chill washes over her. Reflexively she makes a sign of the cross, then tugs at her sweater to button it up. Aside from a few open casket funerals, she hasn't seen a dead person since her first husband, Bobby, died thirty years ago, and that was in a hospital bed. A dead man in a La-Z-Boy chair doesn't make sense.

Howard's glasses have slipped down his nose. He's wearing his Timex watch, khakis, and the tan sneakers Elaine's grandson calls *geezer* shoes. His pale blue shirt is stained with the dried remains of the sunny side-up eggs she'd cooked him for breakfast.

She tries to remember Howard's arms around her. Instead, she thinks of Bobby, his wide smile, his teeth big and white. The tobacco and Aqua Velvet smell of him. She remembers how he towered over her in the doorway of their bedroom to pull her close, bending down to whisper words in her ear, words that made her breath quicken, words that seem unimaginable to her now. How long ago it seems, that time when there was not just the fierce ache of wanting, but of being loved and desired in return.

As she shuts the door behind her, Elaine realizes how sour the den smells, like rotting fruit, and she makes a note to spray it with air freshener. The latch clicks in place. And only then does Elaine begin to weep. It doesn't seem real, Howard gone, Howard dead.

Everything in the kitchen is silent except for the clock on the wall ticking like knitting needles. Time announcing how inescapably it passes. Elaine never drinks in the day, but she opens the cupboard to look for something to steady her nerves. She finds only a bottle of Kahlua. It will do with coffee, near enough to an Irish coffee. She yanks open another cupboard to get out the jar of instant coffee. How long since she's had a real

Irish coffee? She may be misremembering, but she sees herself much younger and thinner, celebrating in a San Francisco bar, perhaps the year Robert passed the bar exam.

After she mixes her drink, Elaine walks toward her outside deck through the living room. There she stops to look at her collection of Hummel figurines, lined up on her corner knick-knack rack: *Celestial Strings, All by Myself, Heavenly Harmony, Retreat to Safety,* and the others, all beautifully fashioned with rose-bud lips, golden waves of hair, doe eyes, and garments of supernal blue, peachy orange, and golden ochre. Something about the figurines recalls for her an innocent, more joyful time. She hasn't dared to buy a Hummel for herself in years because they'd gone up so much in price, and the grief from Howard wouldn't have been worth it. Hummels were kitsch, he said, and what did she see in ugly clay trolls? Why couldn't she collect something more substantial like stamps or antiques or rare books, something of value?

Outside on the second-story deck, Elaine sits in the chaise lounge and listens to bamboo wind chimes clattering in the breeze. The jasmine vines below her sway with delicate ivory blossoms. In the birdbath, a terra-cotta angel kneels with her palms cupped together over a pool of moss-covered water. How comforting, stealing a few minutes to soak up the early afternoon sun with the snow-covered mountains in the distance.

When Howard and she had bought the condominium fifteen years ago, fleeing the cold of Michigan for Southern California where her children had moved, they'd stood on this deck and marveled at the majestic view before them. The mountains loomed in the distance, glittering like a promise of

something unspoiled. She was in her late fifties then, Howard
ten years older. The air around them, Californian air, felt exotic,
perfumed with honeysuckle and magnolia blossoms, the tops
of lemon trees bursting with yellow offerings, splashing against
the rail of their second-story deck. She'd said to him that day,
"Have I told you lately that I love you?" Howard had cleared
his throat and smiled at her.

She'd known by then that her marriage, on the rebound not
long after Bobby's death, had been a mistake. And looking at
those mountains that day, she'd pined for her first husband,
even allowed herself to imagine she might find the courage to
divorce Howard.

She thinks of Howard lying still and cold in the den, and
tries to push from her mind the story of Sue Abbott whose
husband Ralph died in his sleep of a heart attack three months
ago. Two sheriff deputies accompanied the paramedics and
rummaged through the couple's medicine cabinet, quizzing
Sue about what medications her husband had taken, asking if
she'd given him any other pills, and snapping pictures of poor
Ralph and the bedroom, paying particular attention to the
pillow on the floor beside the bed.

Elaine's heart jumps and races like a hummingbird's wings.
She will have to come up with a story. Perhaps she'll simply
say she'd returned from birding, fixed herself lunch and fell
asleep on the deck without checking on Howard, who napped
regularly at this time of day.

A bird warbling, babbling in that chatty way young
songbirds often do, interrupts Elaine's thoughts. Against the
crimson leaves of a plum tree, she sees a flash of yellow, perhaps

an evening grosbeak or an American goldfinch. She reaches for the binoculars around her neck, pushes herself from the lounge chair, and peers over the deck railing for a better look, but the bird flies away too quickly.

Gazing down at the garden below with its pink Splendor zinnias, purple fountain grass, Inca yellow marigolds, and riot of blazing magenta bougainvillea, the tangled colors so enchanting, she doesn't notice the man until he's standing at the birdbath.

It's Mr. Wetherill. He's her age and often wears his pants inside-out with socks but no shoes. He's starting to lose his memory, but no one holds it against him. Many of Sun City's residents are fighting the same battle.

Around the birdbath Mr. Wetherill waltzes in a slow circle, extending his arms as if he's dancing with an unseen partner. He stops at the birdbath, leans over and studies it, perhaps looking for his reflection.

"Mr. Wetherill," Elaine calls down to him.

Mr. Wetherill looks around the garden, confused. It's quite possible he doesn't hear his name, just a noise that doesn't belong to a bird.

Elaine calls him again. Mr. Wetherill looks up and salutes her. "At ease," he says.

"Mr. Wetherill," Elaine says, using the loud voice she puts on for her hard-of-hearing friends. "It's me, Elaine, Elaine Sherman."

"Yes, yes I can see that." Elaine is certain he doesn't know who she is, but he surprises her. "And how is Howard on this fine afternoon?"

"Oh, Howard's the same as he ever is. He's back in the den. Doesn't matter, rain or shine, he's watching television." Elaine's heart flip-flops like a fish out of water. Her fabrication feels strangely liberating.

"Well, give him my regards." Mr. Wetherill turns away to bend again over the birdbath, where he takes off his glasses and places them in the palms of the terra-cotta angel. Then he removes his watch and ring and fumbles behind his ears to detach his hearing aids. He puts them next to his glasses, patting the angel's hands before he opens his mouth to pry out his dentures. With this pile of intimate belongings before him, Mr. Wetherill dips his hands into the mossy water, splashing and rubbing his face, then straightens up and looks around the garden as if he's searching for a towel. He uses his shirttail to pat his face dry before he looks back up toward Elaine, standing at the deck railing watching his strange behavior.

"Tell Howard I picked up the goods he wanted," Mr. Wetherill yells. His voice sounds commanding, a low rumble that suits his former military status. "I'll drop by in a few minutes with them."

"Howard's napping," Elaine answers quickly. "Come another day."

Without his hearing aids he doesn't hear her. He scoops up his belongings and waltzes away. Not to worry, she thinks, Mr. Wetherill will forget their conversation as soon as he leaves the garden.

Elaine unwinds the binoculars from her neck and places them on the low table beside the lounge chair. She sits down and drinks the last of her Irish coffee. It is time to call 911, but she wants just a few more minutes of peace before the commotion of death begins, the calls to her children and his, choosing the casket, deciding on the appropriate service, calling in the obituary, dealing with Social Security and the banks. Elaine remembers the sluggish, frenzied days after Bobby's death.

Howard had the foresight to purchase a burial plot for the two of them, and he insisted that he wanted a plain pine casket and a short graveside ceremony. His daughter will want a full Catholic Mass, but Elaine refuses to think about that quarrel right now. As memorial keepsakes in the casket, she'll put in his favorite snack, a jar of peanut butter and Saltine crackers, a CD of his favorite singer, Frank Sinatra, and the remote control. Elaine smiles to herself. She's being uncharitable but she cannot help it. Howard, once an avid reader who disdained television, died with the remote control in his hand, and that's the narrative she's going to tell.

As the loosening effect of the alcohol ripples through her, Elaine feels in her body now the perplexing mixture of sadness and relief assaulting her, as if battling for dominance. Next week would have been Howard's eighty-second birthday, next month their twenty-seventh anniversary. She cannot believe that she'll never again hear his voice, often gentle, often cajolingly sweet.

The first time she'd seen Howard, he'd been walking through the office while she clacked away at a memo on her typewriter. He was of medium height and compact, a tennis player. His glasses were shoved atop his head, and his bushy eyebrows and brown eyes dominated his face, lined with handsome creases. He carried himself with confidence, though he was known around the office as tightly wound and demanding. Some of the other secretaries thought him disdainful. When he'd stopped at her desk with papers in his hand, he pronounced her name in a way that made her think of herself as someone important, not just another secretary in the pool. And that South Carolina lilt of his, with its hint of good breeding, won her over.

She'd looked up to his crisp blue shirt and paisley tie, his thick grey hair, and graceful hands that might have belonged to a pianist and saw a sophisticated man who might rescue her from her lonely widowhood, give her the happiness she'd known with Bobby. Her children were grown, her house empty of the footsteps clambering up stairs, of the hollering and bursts of laughter.

An impatient knocking disturbs her reverie, and it takes Elaine a moment to realize that someone is at her door. She gets up from her chaise lounge to answer it, expecting to find Marilyn, who lives a few blocks away, but it's Mr. Wetherill holding a bouquet of flowers and a magazine in his hands. Mr. Wetherill has already opened the screen door to knock, and with nothing but space between them, Elaine invites him in. The door to the den is closed, and he wouldn't be so rude as to barrel on back there.

"Howard asked me to get these for you," Mr. Wetherill says, handing the flowers to Elaine.

"Oh, Mr. Wetherill, you must be mistaken, but what a kind gesture."

"I'm not half as daft as people make me out to be," Mr. Wetherill says. "It's the first day of spring, isn't it? I saw Howard this morning. He wasn't looking terribly well, and I asked him if there was anything I could get him. I was about to take the bus over to the mall for a late breakfast and he asked me to buy you flowers."

Howard hasn't given her flowers since her birthday several years ago. Confused, hands trembling, Elaine takes the flowers from Mr. Wetherill. Her voice chokes up when she thanks him, but he doesn't seem to notice.

"Now where is Howard?" Mr. Wetherill asks, shaking the magazine at her. "Your husband needs to read this article. He's lost his senses if he thinks that demagogue is going to represent the Grand Old Party."

"Howard loves baiting people into an argument," Elaine says. "He doesn't like that huckster any more than you or I."

"Well, he sure –

"In any case, you were right, Mr. Wetherill. He was feeling a bit under the weather this morning and went to bed. I'm sorry."

Disappointed, Mr. Wetherill hands Elaine the magazine and says he's pressed back the pages of the article he hopes Howard will read. He leaves muttering that they'll have to have their verbal joust over a game of checkers tomorrow. The magazine in her hand is a Victoria Secret's catalogue.

Elaine puts the flowers in a vase of water in the kitchen and looks at the wall clock. Nearly an hour has passed since she found Howard, and Marilyn still isn't here. Typical. Elaine fixes herself a cup of coffee without the Kahlua and again surrenders herself to the chaise lounge.

Drowsy, she remembers how she'd awakened from her back surgery in the hospital two years ago and found Howard sitting at her bedside, gazing at her with a relieved smile. How his tenderness touched her.

"Were you afraid I wouldn't wake?" she'd asked.

"You looked so lovely sleeping," he'd said, leaning over to brush a strand of hair from her forehead. "Don't ever leave me."

His words had surprised her because even in her drugged state she'd been sure he was alluding to divorce. They never spoke of the discord between them. Instead, they'd settled into a pattern of bickering followed by a sullen silence broken only when one of them made a gesture toward peace. It was her fault just as much as his. Assertiveness is not her strong suit. And Howard was as stingy with affection as he was with money, often as overbearing with her as he'd been with his staff. She'd been too hesitant to push back, and by the time she'd finally admitted as much to herself, her second-bit role as secretary to his boss was cemented as securely as one of her grandchildren's hands in a circle of dried clay, forever diminutive.

Elaine sips her coffee and rubs the fabric of her blouse between her fingers. It's a floral pattern that reminds her of a dress she once owned. Howard had complimented the pattern, told her how pretty she looked in it, and then ruined the moment by saying the dress reminded him of one his ex-wife had worn to their daughter's high school graduation.

It seemed Howard had never really gotten over her. Elaine had been married to him for sixteen years when his best friend let slip that Howard had married and divorced Cynthia twice.

"Why didn't you tell me?" she'd asked, furious that he'd

kept such a secret from her.

"What difference would it have made?"

"But you must have been mad about her to have married her twice!"

"I don't see any reason to bring this up now, all that was years ago," he said, looking at her with exasperation.

"But why did you hide it from me?"

"Don't be absurd. I'm going downstairs to get the mail." He came back half an hour later with the mail and pastries from Elaine's favorite bakery, and she decided to let it go. Howard was right. What was the point after all that time?

A breeze rattles the wind chimes, and Elaine thinks of the faraway day Bobby sat across from her in a wooden rowboat so small and narrow their feet touched. She remembers how the leaves rustling at the shoreline that day sent a whisper up her back and how the muscles in his upper arms rippled as he pulled through the smooth water. How old had they been? Fifteen? Sixteen? When he pulled the boat to shore near a grassy field of buttercups, he'd taken her hand to help her step from the small rowboat, and she'd stumbled. He'd caught her close, brushed back a strand of her hair, and kissed her full and hard on the lips. His mouth, Elaine would always remember, tasted like the peppermint candy he'd shared with her that day.

Perhaps her love for Bobby had rivaled Howard's for Cynthia, and if so, what marriage could thrive under the weight of such unanswered longings? Elaine thinks of all the empty space between Howard and her during their marriage, between their beds, their bodies, their lips and fingertips. No, she thinks, you couldn't live with someone that long and not love him. Perhaps they'd been partners more companionable than passionate, but they'd loved each other in their own clumsy manner.

"Oh, Howard, I will miss you," Elaine whispers, wishing Howard were still alive so that she might say these words to him.

She must have fallen asleep. Someone is shaking her shoulder.

"Elaine," Marilyn murmurs. She's wearing dark sunglasses and a leopard print blouse that shows off her breasts, implants she is inordinately proud of.

"Oh my goodness," Elaine says. "What time is it?"

"I got here as soon as could," Marilyn says defensively, as she sits down on the plastic outdoor chair beside her sister. Her hair is dyed blacker than Elaine has ever seen it, and she wonders if she and Marilyn would look more like sisters if Marilyn deflated her breasts and let her hair go as white as Elaine's.

Elaine looks at her watch. It's two-thirty. Nearly three hours have passed since she found Howard. Marilyn places a brown paper bag tied with a purple ribbon in Elaine's lap.

"You should be more careful," Marilyn says. "Your front door was unlocked. I knocked and you didn't answer, so I tried it and bingo. I suppose we all forget once in a while, but there have been burglaries around here lately."

"Mr. Wetherill dropped by to get Howard," Elaine says, surprised at how easily this lie slips from her tongue. "They left for a game of checkers. Howard must have forgotten to lock it."

Marilyn smiles. Marilyn could care less about two old

men. Marilyn is dating a man seven years her junior, a retired wealthy developer whom she's determined to snare. Elaine's children call Marilyn *The Merry Widow,* even though she's a three-time divorcée.

"I don't want to keep you," Elaine says. "Aren't Tuesdays your nail salon day?"

Marilyn holds up her hands. "I stopped at the nail salon before I came over."

"Of course you did," Elaine says, as she gets up from the chaise lounge with the bag in her hand. "I told you I'm in desperate pain and need your help right away, and you get here in Marilyn time."

"Whoa, no need to get upset," Marilyn says, taking off her sunglasses. "Have you ever been high? Be careful with these treats. Edibles are dicey. I couldn't find my non-psychoactive batch with just CBD oil. These have THC in them, so don't take more than a bite or two, or you might be spaced out for hours, maybe paranoid too, and I won't be able to help you. Since you cancelled, Kenneth and I are going to dinner."

"My goodness aren't you an authority on weed."

"It's medicinal marijuana, not weed, thank you very much."

"Well, no matter, I have things to do," Elaine says, squeezing around Marilyn's chair on the small deck and walking back into her condo with the lunch bag of brownies. "I'll try one later."

"I thought your back was killing you," Marilyn says, following Elaine inside.

"You took so long I took some Advil," Elaine says, not bothering to keep the sharpness out of her voice. "I'll save these for tonight."

Marilyn gives her sister a quizzical look before she snatches the bag from Elaine's hands. "I'm having second thoughts about this," she says. "You seem agitated. I want to make sure you're okay. Why don't we each take a bite of forbidden chocolate? Share the experience. Sisters in arms."

Marilyn is not concerned about Elaine's well-being. Elaine is tired of making excuses for her. Marilyn probably wants what she calls a "mellow buzz." Elaine reaches to grab the brown lunch-bag back, but Marilyn twists away and heads down the hallway.

"I have another UTI," Marilyn calls from the hallway.

Elaine's stomach drops. Ditzy Marilyn, who could be high for all Elaine knows, might open the wrong door. The doors to the den and bathroom are side by side. If she opens the door, Elaine will have to feign shock and they'll call 911 together, and maybe that will be a good thing, having Marilyn at her side if the sheriff's department shows up. Elaine can't decide whether to run down the hall and block the den, or wait to see what Marilyn does. Her indecision paralyzes her. Marilyn returns a few minutes later, complaining about the smell in the hallway.

"I suppose as we get older our sense of smell —"

"I sprayed earlier. I think it's a dead rat in the drainpipe. Are you going to give me the brownies or not?"

Marilyn looks at the lunch bag in her hands and says, "Brew some coffee and we'll share."

"So you want to get high?"

"I'm not a pothead like Bruce," Marilyn snaps.

Elaine's younger son is married with three children. He

has a good job selling software or hardware, Elaine can never remember which, and may still indulge in weed for all Elaine knows, but it has been decades since anyone called Bruce a pothead. "You're a bitch, Marilyn," she says, and not softly.

Marilyn's chest and cheeks turn a mottled red. "What … what?" she stammers. "What has gotten into you?"

Elaine heads for the door, opens it, and says, "Leave."

Marilyn shrugs, lifts her purse from the kitchen counter, and hands Elaine the bag of brownies at the door. "Maybe you should have a bite now. Take the edge off and relax. Then take a nap. You're out of sorts."

"You have no idea," Elaine says, holding the door open for her sister. Marilyn puts her sunglasses on and gives her sister a tight smile before saying goodbye.

With the bag of brownies in her hand, Elaine walks back toward the den feeling giddy. Until she reaches the door. A wave of anxiety and regret sweeps through her as she twists the knob. Howard looks whiter, more waxen, and the den seems colder.

Elaine sets the bag of brownies near the phone. She takes a deep breath. This is too important to bungle. The den is so quiet that she imagines herself aloft, floating in a capsule in space. She takes a step closer to Howard, pulls the afghan puddled at feet on the footrest up to his knees. Next, she opens the drawer to his desk, rummaging through it until she finds his green marbled fountain pen, a gift from his grandfather who ran a stationary and pen shop. Howard often used the pen to write postcards to his daughter and friends back in Michigan. Lifting the remote control from Howard's lap, she replaces it with the pen and a blank postcard of the sun rising under a purpled sky on a California beach. Then she turns toward the desk, unsure and lightheaded at her choice, at the very fact of allowing herself the choice. Which to reach for first, the phone or the brownies?

THE BLIND

JOSEPH ZACCARDI

At a traffic light in the theatre district a castaway sits sideways on the sidewalk on the opposite side of the street I see two holes for eyes a mouth twisted I cross toward her when the light turns green her face wrapped in skin of shadow she's dressed in charity clothes from houses of the poor from houses of the rich from many houses her outstretched hand awaits me in the early morning hour when the sun is low when my shadow is very long every day she reaches out for spare change I drop a few coins and pocket lint try not to touch her try to avoid the vacant glance because her eyeless glance accuses because there's a hint of unease on both sides of this transaction the way two actors in a bad play know they're part of a bad play on this busy street in this busy city where I pay out coins into a hand as though I were feeding a parking meter shamefaced my shadow covers this woman near the gutter cluttered with scraps and street dirt who doesn't know who I am doesn't know my name.

IN THE VALLEY OF WINDOWS

Joseph Zaccardi

In a gradation of gray seams in gray light
there's a crow perched on a power line crowing
I live half my time in thought in the other half try to solve
past mistakes it's not that easy the crow is saying listen
to the morning waken to the night crawlers' retreat
listen to a dog somewhere uphill who barks at shadows
(if you don't have a dog nearby do your own barking)
listen to a man and woman down in the downtown flats
he's saying he won't be home till late and she says
what's the difference when you're here you're not here
how awful it must be to be together and alone
by the time the barking dog has stopped barking
the day begins to emerge to revolve and resolve
the man slams shut his car door fires up the ignition
upshifts and peels out on loose gravel downshifts to a stop
for no answer is an answer for this is about not talking
it's about the curtain that falls between people
the day completes its arc the moon in the right part of the sky
the dog bedded down for the night dreams about squirrels
the crow waits and watches night's cover dissolve
shadows return to their trees

DNA REFLECTS ON DEATH

Charlotte Pence

I cannot offer wisdom about Charon's leaky
row boat cajoling you, swaying you between
the worlds, but I can offer that the wooden floor

is always wet. Boards soft with salt and slosh.
Paint rubbed off by tapping boots. I can offer
that wisdom carries with it blood—despite

attempts to pretend that life doesn't require
the taking of life. That chimps don't plot
their victims' dismemberments. I cannot offer

old stories of the world beginning in a wink
of white or beginning on the back of a sea-green
turtle. I do know how everywhere we see reminders

of what has come before us. That albatross,
white as sin, over our heads. Everywhere birds—
from wharfs to sky rises—twill the air with song,

and still you ask for more song. I can offer that
this thing called heat is a fire that seeks solitude—
crisp neatness of black stubble instead of field.

I can offer that matter trying to tear us apart is neither
dark nor invisible. I can offer that the words
"Come Back" are often the last you'll hear.

DESCENDANT(S)

Liz Prato

On a warm January evening my husband and I lay on the bed of our Lihuʻe hotel room watching *The Descendants*. It was our first viewing, even though the movie had been out for two months and nominated for five Academy Awards. It's weird we hadn't seen it yet for two reasons: One, because I'm obsessed with Hawaiʻi, where *The Descendants* takes place, and usually consume any and everything to do with it, and two, because, duh, George Clooney.

The other reason this scene was weird is because we were in a hotel in Lihuʻe in the first place. Lihuʻe is the administrative capital of Kauaʻi, home to the island's only commercial airport. Lihuʻe is where you can depend on having to wait in a line—at your hotel, at a restaurant, to rent a boogie board, to find a parking space, to eventually make a left turn. It's where cruise ships dock and shuttle passengers to Kmart to buy cheap macadamia nuts and tiki shot glasses and Kona coffee. Lihuʻe is crowded and loud by Kauaʻi standards, so we always stay in Poʻipu, fifteen miles away. But that January afternoon we had arrived at the Lihuʻe Marriott after abandoning the house we were renting in Poʻipu, because the windows in the house either didn't open or didn't close and all had signs warning us to keep them locked, otherwise burglary was likely. We abandoned the house because there was a milky-white stain on the comforter, and even after we moved it to another room I couldn't get rid of the icks. The side of the refrigerator was covered in rust, and the bathroom faucet and tiles covered in scale. The couch was both too hard and too soft, and was made of some waterproof, sunscreen-proof fabric that made me itch. We abandoned the house because the second we walked in—before I knew about the windows or the rust or the comforter or the itch—I immediately sensed bad juju. Some messy weightedness that had been left there by a previous guest or the owners that didn't belong to me and that I couldn't fend off. I wasn't strong enough. I needed to be coddled, comforted, secure.

Five months earlier my bipolar brother, Steve, had died at the age of 45. He suffered two pulmonary emboli in the middle of the night, fourteen months after our dad died. I flew from Portland to Denver for Steve's funeral, held on what would have been my mom's 75th birthday, if my mom were still alive. Three weeks later I returned to Denver and, in one long weekend, cleaned out the house I grew up in, the house Steve and my dad shared. It was 4,000 square feet of detritus collected by two small-time hoarders over forty-five years. My childhood home was in foreclosure because my dad died with massive debt, and it would be auctioned off by the city. I came to Hawai'i only a month out of the subsequent—almost unavoidable—nervous breakdown that almost took me away from this world.

That's why my husband and I were at a hotel in Lihu'e.

The Descendants begins with a montage of real life in Honolulu: high rises, freeway traffic, homelessness, and an old woman reaching up to rub her neck as if trying to rid herself of a deep ache, while George Clooney's character, Matt King, narrates that mainlanders assume he lives in some sort of perpetual paradise where nothing bad happens, where people feel no pain or sickness or suffering simply because they are surrounded by palm trees and waves. He ends the speech with five glorious words: "Paradise can go fuck itself."

The Descendants is based on a novel of the same name by Kaui Hart Hemmings. While adapting it for the screen, Alexander Payne made the story not just more emotionally condensed, but also edgier, while remaining loyal to what the story is about. First, it is about an immediate family: Matt and his wife Elizabeth, their teen daughter Alexandra, and their ten-year-old daughter Scottie. When the movie starts, the family is scattered in vastly different directions emotionally, and in some cases geographically. Matt is immersed in his work and hasn't emotionally engaged with Elizabeth for so long that, he later finds out, she's been having an affair. Alex is a problem teen—drinking, drugs, bad grades and we assume sex—and has been sent to boarding school on the Big Island to straighten her out. Ten-year-old Scottie cusses, watches porn with her friends, and bullies other kids at school. And then Elizabeth has a speed boating accident that puts her in a permanent coma. She has a living will mandating she not be kept alive artificially, so Matt is legally required to pull the plug. This already-fractured family must figure out some way to come together and deal with the new fracture. The permanent fracture, the one that cannot be fixed.

A counselor told me that when my mom died, my family went from being a table with four legs to a table with three legs. Maybe, in some families, the remaining three try to compensate for the missing fourth leg. My family didn't do that. We pretended that fourth leg wasn't missing, or wasn't that important, or that we weren't even one table, since my parents were divorced and Steve and I were both technically "adults" (twenty-eight, and twenty-six, respectively). It felt like my mom and I were one table, Steve and my dad the other, and I had to deal with the brokenness on my own. But less than ten years after my mom died, the systemic instability became apparent and we all started to fall down. My brother's mental illness led to severe physical illness, and my dad, unable to deal with the consequences, repeatedly tried to commit suicide. And then there was me, trying not to implode while my remaining family did.

The Descendants is also about family on a bigger scale: Matt's great great grandmother Ke'alohilani was a Hawaiian princess, one of the last descendants of King Kamehameha the Great. She married her haole (white) banker, and together the power couple amassed thousands of acres of land. As a result, Matt and his extended family own 25,000 acres of undeveloped property on Kaua'i that sits in a trust. The extended family is referred to as "The Cousins"—there are no parents in Matt's family, no aunts or uncles or siblings, and certainly no grandparents. Just like me at the age of forty-four.

While Elizabeth is lying in this permanent coma, The Cousins are days away from voting on who to sell their 25,000 acres to because a law dictates that, in seven years, the trust holding the land be dissolved. While the book doesn't cite any legal reason for the trust's dissolution, Payne and a law scholar he engaged saw this an opportunity to provide some poignant Hawaiian history. Randall Roth, a professor at the University of Hawai'i, advised Payne of the Rule Against Perpetuities, which states that a private trust must be dissolved twenty-one years after the last person involved in the creation of the trust dies. (This is apparently an incredibly convoluted law, so I'm just giving the headlines here.) In general, the RAP is meant to limit how long descendants must abide by a dead person's wishes. The law is particularly resonate in Hawai'i, where vast amounts of land was acquired by the white aristocracy in the 1800's. The RAP means, in theory, that imperialist sugar barons and pineapple barons and sandalwood barons don't get to control Hawaiian land forever.

Most of Matt King's cousins haven't exactly been out there making a living, and are depending on this eventual sale as their cash cow. Matt only lives off the money he earns through his law practice, so that's not his concern. He's also the sole trustee and can basically do whatever he wants. There's tremendous pressure on him to make the "right" decision— not just from The Cousins, but also from the residents of Hawai'i, who have an emotional investment, a spiritual investment, in what happens to this enormous unspoiled parcel of beach and jungle and pasture. Many people don't want him to sell at all, because they don't want to see more shopping malls and golf courses and hotels and condos and traffic on their island paradise. Wherever Matt goes, people ask, "Do you know what you're going to do, yet?"

If there is one fault to this plot, it would have to be that seven years doesn't seem like the most urgent ticking clock in the world. My dad was a real estate developer and named eleven heirs in his will so, trust me, I understand the complications of dividing things like land and stocks among numerous parties. I get that in trying to distribute 25,000 acres of land equitably, someone will inevitably feel ripped-off because they didn't get the beach-front location, or the land with a great view, or whatever signals "value" to them. But I have a hard time believing that a decision that will not only affect the financial solvency of Matt's twenty-four slacker cousins, but also the *entire state* of Hawai'i, has to be made at the exact moment his wife is being taken off life support.

Elizabeth is on life support for the entire movie, except for an opening scene shot without music or dialogue that shows her speeding through the ocean in a powerboat. You only see her from the chest up, giving the sense that she's levitating. Honolulu and Diamond Head are in the background, getting farther and farther away from Elizabeth with each second. She not only looks happy in this short scene; she looks content. A few times in my life I have thought, "I could die right now and I'd be happy"—like, when I saw the Eiffel Tower light up and sparkle at night. But in times when I have felt content, when my body and soul feel at rest—usually when I am near an ocean, the Pacific Ocean, Kaua'i—I want to stay in that place forever. Although Elizabeth is described as some sort of "thrill-seeker," that's not what the opening scene tells me. She wanted to feel wanted by the world, to belong to it. It's why she's having an affair. It's why she's speeding on a boat with the sun and salt-water spraying her face.

Except for during that short whiff of contentedness, we only see Elizabeth in a hospital bed, in a coma, breathing labored, eyes closed. When my mom was in a coma, her eyes were open, sort of rolled back into her head. At one point, a kind nurse closed them. She also dotted Vaseline on my mom's lips. As Elizabeth nears death, rolled-up washcloths are placed in her fists to keep her hands from contorting into claws and digging into her own palms. My mom never had the washcloths because it was only 24 hours between when she slipped into the coma and when she died. For Elizabeth King, it was almost a month.

Not surprisingly, several parties are interested in the King family's 25K acres. One of the leading bids is from a Chicago developer who has offered an astounding half a billion dollars. There's another bid from a guy named Holitzer that isn't for quite as much—but still reasonable —but is favorable because he's from Kaua'i. Sort of. He's a Kaua'i-born boy who went on to make a fortune in Silicon Valley, an allusion to AOL co-founder Steve Case, who was born in Honolulu and now owns 40,000 acres on Kaua'i. Most of The Cousins want to sell to Holitzer because at least the ownership and money comes from and stays in state. This is *kind of* conscientious, and shows sort of an understanding of the complexity of outside ownership. Never mind that Holitzer is haole, not Hawaiian, and still intends to build resorts and golf courses— and very well might hire mainland developers to do so. But The Cousins' perspective represents a very real one for some residents of Hawai'i—haole and otherwise: the land is there, tourism is a major industry, lots of money is nice to have, so why not just rip up the kukui and koa and monkeypod trees?

Like the Northern Spotted Owl became a symbol of deforestation in the Pacific Northwest, the Monkeypod tree is the poster child for the political, cultural and environmental concerns surrounding tourist development on Kaua'i. Old Kōloa Town, adjacent to the resort community of Po'ipu, is lined with shops and restaurants in original planation buildings that have been restored and renovated. The area was long known for the forty monkeypod trees providing a great canopy of shade for the buildings. Then, in 2008, a Michigan developer called The Nelsen Companies moved ahead on a plan to build a brand! New! Strip! Mall! in Old Kōloa Town. Their first step was bulldozing seventeen historic monkeypod trees. Residents weren't happy. *We* weren't happy—and we're tourists, for god's sake. But we're the kind of tourists who go to Hawai'i to get away from strip malls, who don't want to see the character of a historic town decimated for redundant retail outlets. (The tenants committed to the Shops at Kōloa included a grocery store—even though there is one 250 feet in one direction and another 500 feet in the other direction; an American Savings Bank, even though First Hawaiian Bank is just down the block; a shave ice store, even though there's already one around the corner . . . you get the picture). The most heinous of the promised tenants was an ABC, one of a chain of seventy-eight stores that sells cheap puka necklaces, plastic leis, printed t-shirts, cellophane grass hula skirts, calendars of bikini-clad local women, toy 'ukuleles, and pineapple-shaped serving dishes made from monkeypod wood.

There were protests before the monkeypod trees were bulldozed, and after they were bulldozed, and it seems all for naught: eight years later, absolutely no building has commenced. Construction stalled over permit and financing problems. At least two of the stores originally committed to tenancy have backed out, further obstructing the developer's ability to finance the project. It sounds like another story of a mainland developer barging in and trying to bulldoze paradise to make big bucks, until you dig a little. That's when you find that The Nelsen Companies was simply contracted by the actual owner of the land. The owner of the land is the Eric A. Knudsen Trust, and Eric A. Knudsen is a descendant of a West Kauaʻi sugarcane baron who was married to Anne McHutcheson Sinclair, who was the daughter of Elizabeth Sinclair, who purchased the island of Niʻihau from King Kamehameha V for $10,000 in gold in 1864. Her descendants still own Niʻihau and maintain it as a private homeland for Native Hawaiians where there are no hotels, no stores, no paved roads and no visitors allowed unless they have been expressly invited by an island resident. Although Elizabeth Sinclair's descendants—and Eric Knudson's—are haole, they have lived on and protected the land, the ʻāina, for one hundred and fifty years—just like Matt King's family. Which is to say, the people who decided to plow down those monkeypod trees to make way for an ABC Store are not mainland bad guys. They're not the heroes of the story, either, but, like Matt King's cousins, they have a complicated relationship to the 'āina, and not a clear compass dictating what to do with it.

My dad was one of those mainland developers. The reason I spent so much time in Hawai'i as a teen is because he was building a housing subdivision on Maui. It never occurred to me, not until well into adulthood, that he might be considered a bad guy. That he was another haole tearing up trees and draining precious resources and contributing to Hawaiians getting further away from their 'āina. The land was there, people needed housing, and I got to go to Hawai'i two or three times a year—that's what mattered to me.

To the best of my knowledge, the subdivision was never completed. We stopped going to Maui as a family, but in my youthful arrogance I assumed it was because Steve and I were adults and had our own lives. When I cleaned out my dad and brother's house, I found no partnership papers or blueprints for the subdivision, no proof it ever existed. I remember my dad complaining about how slow and difficult the permitting process was on Maui. Perhaps, like the Shops at Kōloa, the whole thing just stalled out, my dad sold the land, and that was the end of his involvement with the 'āina.

Like all good plots, *The Descendants* has a complication. In this case it's—wait for it—Matt discovering that Elizabeth's lover stands to profit greatly from the sale to Holitzer through real-estate commissions. As you might imagine, Matt is not super-psyched to put money in that guy's pocket. But he also recognizes that Holitzer's bid is a good bid, and is the wish of the people he represents: The Cousins. But is that really who he represents? The camera spends a lot of time spanning over black and white photos of his ancestors, from his brown-skinned great great grandmother wrapped in orchid leis, to her white husband, and their increasingly white children, leading up to Matt's parents. For some inexplicable reason, none of these descendants of the Hawaiian princess married Hawaiians. The family has almost completely bred out their Hawaiian blood. And yet they own Hawaiian land.

Matt is acutely aware of that small drop of Hawaiian blood still pumping through his heart, and what it connects him to. This is something I will never quite understand, since my ancestors are a mystery to me. That's how it is for people adopted during the closed-records era: we went through life legally prohibited from knowing the names of our ancestors. We have no pictures of people who look like us. Even if we do somehow manage to obtain our records, if we finally manage to find a picture of someone who looks like us, that doesn't mean those people whose blood pumps through our hearts will want anything to do with us. It doesn't mean they will tell us who else we are descendant of. It's easy enough to say that my lineage is the ancestors of the adoptive mom and dad who raised me, of Jan and Pete Prato, but that's not how it works. DNA is powerful. Blood is powerful. It is what sustains us, feeds us, keeps us alive. DNA is what ties us to lives lived long before we were born.

In one of those coincidences that we think can only happen in movies, Matt finds out that Brian Spear, the guy Elizabeth was having an affair with, is vacationing in Kaua'i, the location of the hotly contested land. Matt takes his family—which has acquired a bonus child, the teenage boyfriend/best friend of Alex, proving comic relief and slacker wisdom—to

Kauaʻi to track down Brian. He's not tracking down Brian
to beat the shit out of him, but to give him the opportunity
to return to Oʻahu and say goodbye to Elizabeth. Okay, that
stretches plausibility a little, that anyone could be *that* nice of
a guy, especially one who's been essentially ignoring his wife
for years. But the true suspension of disbelief is that Matt flies
his daughters to another island while their mother is dying
(His youngest doesn't even know that Elizabeth was removed
from life support). Matt couldn't just call the guy Elizabeth
was sleeping with? No, he wants to see Brian's face. From
that perspective, Matt's not such a nice guy, but an incredibly
selfish guy.

You know what I did when my mother was dying? I sat
by her bed. I watched *Star Trek: Next Generation* while Steve
narrated. "It's an episode with Q, Mom," he said. "One of
your favorites." I called my uncle to tell him his sister was
dying. I sang "What I Did for Love" from Chorus Line to
her. When the priest said we needed to tell her it was okay to
let go, I told my mom it was okay to let go. I went home and
tried to sleep. When the phone rang at 2:00 am to tell me
she was slipping away, I returned to the hospital. My mom
got stronger as soon as we arrived, so Steve and I decided
maybe she couldn't die with us there. That she knew it would
be too hard on us. So we each said goodbye to her and went
home. When I woke up at 10:00 am I called the hospital and
found out there'd been no change. My best girlfriend, the
only person my age I knew who'd lost a parent, took me out
to lunch. We talked about death, because we could. When I
got home I called the hospital and my mom was still alive,

but not alive. In a coma. Never to come out. And I realized she needed me there to die. What I did was get in my car and speed across town and hope to not get a ticket, and I got into bed with my mom and I put my arms around her and held her until she took her last breath. Fifteen minutes—that's how long it took from when I got in bed with her, until then. The last moment. The last breath. That's what I did when my mom was dying. It's impossible to imagine being an airplane ride—no matter how short—away, walking on the beach or listening to a ʻukulele band at Tahiti-Nui in Hanalei when my mom could be taking her last breath.

This is another reason that it was weird that my husband and I were watching *The Descendants* in our hotel room in Lihuʻe, five months after my brother died, a year and a half after my dad died, eighteen years after my mom died, a month after I considered joining them. You'd think that watching a mom—anyone, really—die would not be that great for my mental health. But somehow it was okay. It was okay because I was in Kauaʻi and I believed the land and water would take care of me. If I had watched this movie on the mainland, I would have felt bereft, cut-off, separate from the ʻāina where I feel most content, when my body and soul feel at rest. But in Lihuʻe, I knew the next day I could walk into the water and feel the sun and the wind and the salt-spray against my face. I could feel alive.

Towards the end of the film, Matt delivers a speech that rivals the "paradise can go fuck itself" opening. He tells The Cousins, "We didn't do anything to own this land—it was entrusted to us. Now, we're haole as shit and we go to private schools and clubs, and we can barely speak pidgin, let alone Hawaiian, but we've got Hawaiian blood, and we're tied to this land. And our children are tied to this land."

Matt seems to get it—not just that the clues to who we are and what we should do lie in our blood. He gets that for a hundred and fifty years his white ancestors have been in possession of something that does not rightly belong to them. It's not even that it rightly belongs to Native Hawaiians, either. Native Hawaiians believe that we belong to the land— not the other way around. It is not ours to own, but under the principle of aloha 'āina it's our responsibility to take care of, to nurture and protect the land. Matt's white ancestors changed this attitude by their very presence. Land—territory—was something they conquered and acquired.

Some scholars of Hawaiian history are quick to remind people that the kings and chiefs of the 1800s played a major role in ceding land to the white folks. Elizabeth Sinclair, for instance, didn't steal Ni'ihau from the Kingdom of Hawai'i. Kamehameha V willingly sold it to her. But just as white people brought Christianity and literacy and venereal disease to the Native Hawaiians, they also brought capitalism. They brought the idea that things—most especially land—equal power. And once capitalism inserts itself into the DNA of a culture, it's hard to go back. It turns out people like having the ability to acquire things to make their lives better, or more pleasurable, or whatever their metric is. Governments like having the power that producing and importing and exporting goods affords them. It's one thing if an indigenous culture has never been exposed to any of that. But as soon as the exportation of sugar and sandalwood and pineapple and whale oil became a part of the tapestry of Hawaiian life in the 1800's, it became likely that pulling out those threads would cause a great unraveling. This remains the dilemma of modern Hawai'i. Tourism has grown, and sustained, and destroyed Hawai'i. No matter how theoretically desirable reversing course may seem, it is impossible to go back.

Matt decides not to accept either of the bids—Holitzer's or the half-billion dollars—pointing out that they have seven years to figure out how to keep the land (no kidding!). Cousin Hugh, the "lead" cousin, warns him that they're not intimidated that Matt's a lawyer and will sue his ass. Hugh is a trust fund beach bum, but even before this threat, Beau Bridges plays his supposedly laid-back character with perfectly malevolent undertones. In an earlier scene at Tahiti-Nui, Hugh calls his cousin "Matty," and "Matty Boy," reminding him that all The Cousins want to sell to Holitzer (all of them don't). "You do too, Matty," Hugh delivers with a stern glare, reducing Matt to a child and robbing him of his autonomy, much like the original keepers of this land, the Hawaiians, were robbed of theirs.

It's a brilliant interpretation of character, the kind of guy who knows the bartender's first name—and probably just enough about her personal life to ask questions that make him appear thoughtful—and buys other people drinks and is all "hey, whatever, man" only because someone else is bankrolling his carefree lifestyle. But he's aware that the lifestyle, and the aura it provides him, doesn't belong to him. It belongs to this relative who lives in Honofuckinglulu and tucks his aloha shirt into the khaki pants he wears with a belt and believes he's so high and mighty because he actually has an income-producing career.

My brother was like this. Just replace "beach bum" with its mainland synonym: "guy who hangs out at the golf club." My brother received half the profits of my dad's land deals under the guise of working for him. But mostly what Steve did was stay out until three in the morning at bars, sleep until noon, then go to the Cherry Creek Country Club and maybe play a round, but mostly sit in the bar and buy drinks for his friends. He told women that the house he and my dad lived in was *his* house, and he was letting our dad live there. He told these women our dad actually lived in Canada, and just came to visit sometimes. He told women these lies because he knew that a grown man living with and being supported by his father was pathetic. I also think a part of him believed these falsehoods in order for his ego to survive. Every once in a while my dad appeared to briefly grow a pair and tell Steve that he had to move out. Once he threatened to cut Steve off financially. Steve was so aware that nearly every aspect of his presumed being was based on this illusion, so helpless to what would become of him without it, that he threatened, more than once, to beat up my dad. My dad never made him leave.

Matt and his daughters return to Honolulu to be with Elizabeth. A counselor explains to Scottie that her mother is going to die, while Matt, Alex, and their gray-haired doctor watch with compassion. My attention gets really split at this point in the movie, and an argument could certainly be made that it's because I don't want to be emotionally present in this scene, the one that reminds me of when the doctor told me my comatose mom had no more than twenty-four hours to live. But what I focus on is that the counselor is white. Throughout the entire movie, I've been well aware that brown-skinned locals are only used as background scenery. Yes, this is the story of a haole family—that's inherent in the plot—but why are there so few brown-skinned people in their orbit? In Honolulu, white people make up only 23% of the population, but the doctor, the counselor, the nurses, all of the Kings' friends, Alex's boyfriend and boarding school RA . . . they're white. The few *super minor* speaking roles that go to brown-skinned people are: two grade-school teachers, the girl Scottie bullied (she says two words), the girl's mother, the bartender at the Tahiti-Nui (who also says two words and doesn't even get a screen credit), Alex's roommate, and one other friend of Scottie's. There's a local band playing Hawaiian music at the Tahiti-Nui, and it can be argued that this gives screen time to traditional Hawaiian culture, or that it depicts Hawaiians performing for the entertainment of white folks, robbing them of any sovereign dignity. I assure you there are advocates firmly for each camp, and I feel too much of an outsider, too *haole,* to decide which is "right."

I am not, however, too haole to find this whitewashing entirely maddening. It's a persistent Hollywood malady to set movies in Hawai'i for the scenery, for the exoticism, and yet to exclude the people of Hawai'i, as if they have nothing to do with what Hawai'i is. Local people are, at best, set decoration. At the worst, locals are played by very white actors, either in brown face (Rob Schneider in *50 First Dates*), or without the pretense at all (Emma Stone as a quarter-Chinese/quarter-Hawaiian character with the last name "Ng" in *Aloha*). To set a movie in Hawaiʻi and exclude the people of Hawaiʻi further reinforces the view that their world, their land, their *lives* are simply products for white mainlanders to commoditize. It further attempts to divorce them from their ʻāina.

In the penultimate scene in *The Descendants,* Matt and his daughters bob in a canoe in the calm waters in front of Waikīkī, preparing to spread Elizabeth's ashes, to return her to the place where she was the most content. Unlike the first scene where Elizabeth speeds further away from Honolulu with each passing second, Matt and his girls simply float in one place. They get no closer, but no further away from the land. The girls take turns gently placing a scoop of their mother's corporeal remains into the ocean, and then Matt dumps in the rest. They place leis—the quintessential symbol of the Aloha spirit—in the water to float away with Elizabeth.

I remember riding in the passenger seat while Michael drove us to my dad's funeral, the urn cradled on my lap. This is what becomes of a parent, I thought. My mom's ashes were scattered over Half Moon Bay in California. I'm not entirely sure why, but guess it's because she and my dad travelled there when they were young in their marriage, and she also visited Steve when he was at San Francisco State. None were reasons that had anything to do with me. But that's what it was like back then. Steve and my dad were in charge. I was too bereft, they assumed I was too young, to handle the details of death. Seventeen years later, my life was about nothing but the details of death.

In the last scene of *The Descendants* the camera remains fixed in one place: on the couch in front of the TV, as if the camera and the TV are one in the same. Scottie is curled up underneath a pineapple-colored Hawaiian quilt that had been on her mother's deathbed. She's watching the TV, which emits Morgan Freeman's familiar voice narrating *March of the Penguins*. Matt enters the scene carrying two bowls of ice cream—strawberry for her, mocha chip for him; one a flavor for a child, the other for an adult. He joins Scottie under the quilt as Freeman talks about how isolated Antarctica is, and how, once upon a time, it was tropical. Like Hawai'i.

Alex emerges in the background. She sees her remaining family on the couch, and stands behind them just long enough to let the viewer realize she is deciding whether she will be a part of this family, or will contribute more to its fracturing. She sits next to her father on the couch, under the quilt, and Matt hands her his bowl of mocha chip to share. It's creepy, in a way, how Alex shares the grown-up flavor of ice-cream with Matt as if they are now a couple. Not that anything incestuous is implied, but this young woman, who has barely had time to figure out who she is, who she wants to be, is elevated to the position of eldest woman in the house. You hear these stories all the time, about the mother who died young and the teen daughter who stood in for her and raised her younger sister, who had to abandon her own youth for familial responsibilities.

It took a while until I had to fill that role. I was already an adult when my dad and brother were plunged into their mental and physical illnesses, so trying to care for them theoretically didn't cost me my youth. But they spurned all my attempts to make them better—therapy, addiction treatment, skilled nursing, separation. They were swirling in a Charybdisian maelstrom and wanted to grasp onto me, even if it meant me disappearing into the vortex with them. While Alex could stand behind her father and sister and realize she had the chance to complete something wanting to be whole, my only option for survival was to stand witness as my dad and brother were devoured. But, like Alex, it deprived me of whatever remnants of innocence and youth I'd been clinging to.

We know the King family has money, and can afford a housekeeper or nanny or therapist, or whatever else Scottie needs—other than her mother. Matt will spend less time at work, and Alex probably won't go back to boarding school, so they can all be together. And because Matt refused to sell the land, they can go to Kaua'i whenever they want. They can feel the sunshine on their skin and the salt water in their face, and in those moments, they will remember they are alive.

MORNING OF MY 56TH BIRTHDAY

Andrea Potos

The lake is a blue scarf ironed
by stillness, locust leaves burnt
yellow, everywhere, softness
in September air.
Spread on my table, a book of Keats' letters:

    The first thing that strikes me on hearing
a misfortune having befalled another is:
Well it cannot be helped——he will have
the pleasure of trying the resources of his spirit

    while miles away at this moment, my mother
meets with the doctor. He will aim one perfect
arrow of light in the errant spot that would claim
her if it had its way, my mother
from whose body I came.

HER LAST HOUR

Andrea Potos

We arrived early at ICU,
the kind hospitalist said her chances
had gone from 10% to less than 1%, the time
is now, he said, this breathing is the end
of life breathing, loud and large like the rise
and fall of a boat on swelling waters
carrying her out and away, though from then on
I would plant myself on the shore of each day looking
for signs——there—sometimes, the flash of a sail that shone
like a smile, or the wave of a great fin, appearing, then not.

CHINCOTEAGUE

Joanne Rocky Delaplaine

Now the sea swallows a madder sun.
So much is round: Eleanor's belly, still soft
from giving birth; Asa's head, fists, eyes;
his mouth clamped on her breast, sucking.
Waves lap the shore. Here, at low tide
below the pier, fiddler crabs dart in and out
of holes burrowed in the mud, their clicks
recall typing class, summer, junior year,
fingers pecking keys, our hard, gawky shells.
I watch a male whose yellow-gold front claw
seems useless, something he drags, hauls until
he pauses, raises it like a warning flag, then woos
a female, follows her down a hole backside first,
withdrawing his huge claw last, closing the door.

HOSTILE ADVANCES

Richard Farrell

You notice the woman's luggage first: Adrienne Vittadini, four bags in total, from the *Jacard* collection, like a family of well-heeled prep-school kids lined up next to her on the curb as she waves her hand at your approaching windshield. Her fucking tote bag costs more than you'll make in a month of Thursdays driving this airport limo around Logan.

Something about this woman looks familiar. Flowing bangs, big blue eyes, a blaze of freckles across wide cheeks, a dimpled chin. She's still beautiful, though no longer young. You slow down until she reaches for the handle on her leather roller. Then you punch it. The van races away, and her fist comes down in the rearview.

This isn't a game to you, but a cosmic realignment of the forces of right and wrong. Mindy never understood that. Mindy accused you of being immature. But what you're doing is imparting a lesson, reminding another beautiful woman, with her $2,000 luggage—hand-stitched by malnourished children in South-Asian sweat shops—that, today, the van stops when you say it does.

On the second lap into the Terminal-A departure garage, the woman's still waving. She's inched her fancy luggage closer to the curb. Twenty yards out, you give her a nod, and she replies with more frantic gestures. Then her cell phone comes out, no doubt to complain that the van she's hired is about to go around a second time. Well, Miss Nibs, keep calling and waving. You might go around five times!

On the way in for the third lap, the dispatcher finally calls. "Cut the shit Walker. I'm serious."

This time, you'll stop, and allow this woman to drag her bags toward the van. "I thought you were never going to stop," she says.

Rule One: never apologize. Flash her that grin, equal parts charm and disgust, a grin that says you're not impressed by her designer luggage or her eyes, eyes so blue that they're almost silver.

Load her fancy bags into the van. Help her inside. She smells wonderful, like a forest floor in October mixed with hints of berry and vanilla. It's hard to concentrate because she smells so good and because her eyes are so fucking blue. Where have you seen her before? Who is she? Why can't you remember her name?

"How far west do you go?" she asks.

It's an odd question. Who hires a van service without knowing in advance where that van stops? Her question throws you a little.

"I need to get to the Berkshires," she says. "My regular ride cancelled."

"Everyone's too chickenshit with the snow coming," you say.

"Look. I'm going to Great Barrington. If you'll take me, I'll make it worth your while."

"Out of the question," you say. "Against company policy."

Since when have you cared about company policy? You break three company rules before crawling out of bed. Is your license even valid? This isn't about company policy. It's about the fact that this lady's luggage costs more than your last car.

"A rule follower," she says. "I can respect that. A bit predictable though."

Don your mirrored sunglasses, turn on the heat, and depart the parking garage. Jets, bound for all the over world, taxi and takeoff into ash-colored skies as you drive into the dark tunnel that leads out of Logan.

Mindy has broken your heart. This is an undeniable fact. Though she promised to stick with you through tough times, she split at the first sign of trouble. You're all but certain she's sleeping around. You've thought about slashing her tires, about mauling her cat, about killing her. But the rage has mostly passed. In fact, tonight you've invited Mindy to dinner after work, and you've promised to open a bottle of nice wine. Ribeyes are defrosting in the sink, and you've put fresh sheets on the bed. If tonight goes well, maybe next week you'll take her to Nantucket, where, five years ago, you proposed on the beach. So what if Mindy has only agreed to dinner in exchange for your signature on the divorce papers? You know she hasn't spoken to a lawyer yet, and doubt the $139, online divorce decree is legally binding.

As you approach Newton, the woman starts trying to arrange rides from Worcester to Great Barrington. This goes on for several minutes, and based on the exasperated sighs coming from the back seat, you know the search isn't going well. No one wants to drive with a blizzard on the way.

"Seems strange that you'd climb in a van without knowing where it stops," you say.

She asks your name. You lie and tell her your name is Paul.

"You like this work, Paul?" she says.

"It pays the bills," you say.

In the mirror, she smiles. You stare at her a moment before you see it. Her left bicuspid is chipped. And not just a little chipped, it's a full-on hockey-player ding.

"Don't they have dentists in Beverly Hills?"

"What?" she says. "What did you say?"

"My soon-to-be ex-wife says I lack conventional filters."

"Smart girl," the woman says. "How'd you know I'm from L.A.?"

Don't tell her you recognized her luggage. Don't tell her that, after three years of driving this route, you can read a person's history by their travel attire. Don't tell her that you know what time the big jets land from overseas, what time the shuttles arrive from Reagan and JFK.

She leans forward and you smell again forest-floor and vanilla and glance at her blue eyes.

"Don't be a jerk. I'm going to Great Barrington. Will you take me or not?"

"I've seen you before."

"How much?" she asks.

"It's not about money. I told you, we have regulations."

She shakes her head stares out the window.

"Your ex-wife got out just in time."

Then it hits you, like a lightning bolt from a clear blue sky. You know exactly who the woman is. A chill shivers your spine.

"*Animal House!*"

"Bingo," she says.

You try to recall her name by her movies: *Raiders of the Lost Ark, Scrooged, Starman* and *Sandlot,* a few cameos in Law & Order. She wasn't a big star. She was easy to miss. What the hell is her name? Kate something. No. Not Kate. Katie.

"You're Karen Allen," you say.

"I am," she says. "And I need a ride to Great Barrington."

In *Animal House,* she played the fraternity president's girlfriend, the good girl trying to keep the Delta Tau Chi parties in check, a voice of reason in argyle socks and a cable-knit sweater, gracefully floating above the debauchery. Did she show her breast on the big screen? A flash of her cotton panties? She was the quintessential girl-next-door—two parts innocence, one part raw sexual charm. You tell her it broke your heart a bit when she smoked dope and slept with the hippie English professor played by Donald Sutherland.

"Do you know how many times I hear that?" she says. "Fucking Donald Sutherland ruined me!"

You both laugh as flakes of snow glisten in your headlights. You should be home, drink in hand, heating up the grill, waiting for Mindy

"What happened with your ex?" Karen asks.

"Who the hell knows?" you say. "Women are an inexplicable mystery."

"And men," she says. "Men make so much more sense."

Around the 495 interchange, the Pike traffic bogs down. Low, gray clouds prowl the horizon. The temperature is dropping. There might be three feet of snow by tomorrow. Red lights dash and swerve in and out of lanes, trying to eke out a few extra feet of advantage.

"All these techie assholes," you say. "Rushing home to their little mansions."

"Is there anyone you like?" Karen asks.

She laughs and stares out the window.

"Are you going to take me all the way or not?"

"The tooth," you say. "Tell me about the tooth and we can talk about how far I'll take you."

"I'm not telling you about my tooth," she says. "I'd rather walk home."

Snow begins to stick on the median. Has Karen noticed? What would it be like to sit with her by a roaring fire, the snow falling outside? Would she tell you stories about famous actors, Bill Murray, Harrison Ford, John Belushi?

"Take me to Great Barrington," she says. "I'll pay you two hundred bucks and buy you a beer before you go back."

"Sorry," you say. "I've got plans tonight."

"The ex?" she asks. "Cancel the plans. Have a beer with me in Great Barrington. How often does that happen?"

An odd silence follows. Karen must register the awkwardness too, because she sits back and closes her eyes.

The traffic stays thick for awhile and then suddenly lets up, like a great plug has been removed from a stuck drain. Soon you are driving at full speed.

A moment later, she taps your shoulder and offers a handful

of parmesan-dusted crackers.

"I'm sorry if I said too much," she says. "I have a history of overstepping."

You toss a few crackers into your mouth. "Stale," you say.

"You're full of opinions," she says.

She explains about her two divorces, about custody battles and the saga of aging in an industry that reveres youth and beauty. She points at her lip. "Believe it or not, I don't remember," she says. You glance at her in the mirror, and she smiles wide. "I woke up the other day and the goddamn tooth was chipped."

"You're right," you say. "I don't believe you."

"We're trapped together," she says. "Why can't you just be nice?"

"Your career," you say. "It didn't really blossom."

She laughs. "I'm getting advice from a van driver? That's great. You know what, you can drop me off at the next exit."

Karen sounds angry but says nothing as you zoom past an exit ramp. Instead, she hands you more crackers. A moment later, she leans forward. You can smell her perfume, almost feel her hair against your shoulder.

"Paul, I lied about my tooth," she says. "It's embarrassing, but I'll tell you if you promise not to laugh."

Her evasions are as adorable as her freckled cheeks and her lagoon-blue eyes. You wonder how old she is now. Why wasn't she a bigger star? She's beautiful, as beautiful as dozens of actors with more credits. You're as baffled by her as you are by the moon.

"I was drunk," she says. "I don't drink like I used to. But I was having fun, you know? Just letting my hair down a bit."

You imagine her bronze skin on a bright California beach, with Spielberg and Lucas nearby, a bonfire, strumming guitars, crashing surf.

"I get cravings when I drink," she says. She elongates her words: cravings, drink. Elocution classes. Voice coaches. Method acting workshops. You grew up poor and have had to scrap for every penny. Her story wanders off into the Hollywood hills, but you've stopped listening.

"Your life, has been one giant party. Hasn't it?"

"Jesus," she says, "is it so hard for you to be decent?"

She expects life to be polite and predictable. Mindy was the same—so certain the world owed her. Hell, maybe you thought that too once. When did it all go wrong? Mindy wants someone with more *ambition*. The word chokes in your throat. You had plenty of ambition once. Now you wrestle with rent payments, alimony, your mother's doctor bills. Mindy doesn't care hard you work, how much bullshit you have to swallow on a trip. She wants beach parties, strumming guitars, and fancy luggage.

"I'll take you," you say. Karen either doesn't hear you or is ignoring you now.

"Wait," Karen says. "You haven't let me finish. I wasn't drunk. I'm lying again."

She begins to tell another long, complicated story about a botched crown, a root canal and porcelain cap. She rambles on about various dentists, about anesthesia allergies and dry socket infections. You wonder if it's all an act, if she's rehearsing, trying to get into character. You wonder if her tooth is really chipped, or if it's some Hollywood special effect.

"So I look in the goddamn mirror and I was like, holy hell. My tooth is cracked."

She laughs loudly at her own story, no doubt used to people hanging on her every word. Accustomed to walking into a room and people staring. She expects accolades, parties, ball gowns, and rides home. Not tonight though.

"I'm getting off here," you say. "I'll drop you at the Worcester Airport. You can get a ride from there easy enough."

"You aren't taking me?" she asks. "I thought you would."

"Not tonight," you say.

You tell Mindy all of this while snow swirls and a northeast wind howls. She's barely taken off her jacket, hasn't touched her steak, and has only sipped her wine. She listens to your story, but is not exactly buying it.

"You just love to screw with people," Mindy says.

"That's not the point," you say. "Jesus, are you ever on my side?"

"I need you to sign these papers," she says. "I want this to be over."

"That's it?" you ask. "That's your response to my story?"

"It was Karen Allen," Mindy says. "It's not like it was Meryl Streep."

It hits you then, the extent of your stupidity. You could've driven Karen Allen home. You could've been a nice guy. Maybe she would've bought you a drink. Maybe you could've seen her again. It's not impossible. At the very least, you would've earned some extra cash.

"Let's go to Nantucket next weekend," you say. "Let's just get away together."

"What?" Mindy says. "I'm not going to Nantucket."

Mindy reaches for the wine glass.

"What happened to her tooth?" Mindy asks.

You wonder if Karen would've really bought you a beer.

"You can't drive home," you say. "It's starting to stick out there. You hate driving in the snow."

Mindy slams the rest of her wine. Maybe the night will end well after all. Maybe she'll go to bed with you, rekindle something that's missing.

"No big deal," Mindy says. "A friend is picking me up."

"What kind of friend picks a woman up in a blizzard?" You regret your question as soon as you ask it.

A gust of wind rattles the window. For a moment, the rage returns. Then you think about Karen Allen. You hope she made it home. You hope, in some small way, she's thinking about you tonight. Mindy's phone dings. Headlights beam through falling snow. She buttons her coat. The divorce papers are still sitting on the table. You grab a pen, scribble your signature on the dotted lines, and shove them at her.

"I hope you choke on them," you say.

Mindy leaves without saying goodbye. The house quiets. You open a beer, throw a piece of cold steak into the microwave, and turn on the TV.

You find the DVD scattered amongst a pile in the cabinet. It's scratched, but the machine seems not to care. Ten minutes into the movie, Karen appears, as close now as she was a few hours ago. You can almost smell her skin, hear her voice, taste the parmesan crackers. In the movie, she's wearing a flannel shirt and tending bar in the frat house basement. She offers a beer to one of the pledges and smiles. Then Karen Allen disappears.

ANOTHER MORNING

Sean Sam

Lost, how it fumbles, the boar bleating
until forceps of steel lick its leg, saliva
bleeding thick enough for beetles to bond

in its sap, devoured by formality, bound
as suddenly as the tip of the trap
its snap, yawning white and wide,

a ritual opens its mouth to sigh,
content in procedure while the animal
thrashes and turns, suffers and moves.

Soon part of me will come to this clearing,
another creature without choice, uncovered
as any hunter when bared. The boar slouches

into death, near me, where nothing of sympathy
can reach and what remains to see is the green
in the trees, everything violent exposed

and not judged, the flesh of it flayed,
guts roped into dirt as worms, my needs
broken off bone. The wind whips the grass.

JUPITER AND CHAPARRAL

Lynn McGee

When my sister visited New York,
we waited for the subway and stood watching
down the tunnel for its growing light.
She seemed out of place, I thought,
in her pastel blouse
and full skirt — but she was completely
at ease, noticing the tile from another century,
the train's gathering roar — and I like
to think of her with that ease,

taking in beauty on her last day,
a few years later, clouds soaked
with pink and field electric,
silver crackling across its face.
Her windows were open,
air sweet as her car lumbered
off-road, arms limp in her lap,
concrete blocks breaking
her speed.

Then fangs in her temples withdrew —
she and I would have marveled

at how the body can remember itself
long enough to step from a car
with shredded tires
and be eased down to a quilt
spread on gravel
by a woman who pulled over
to help,
there at the corner of Jupiter
and Chaparral —
Jupiter, god of the sky;
Chaparral, brush-covered Earth —

and our lost girl suspended
between them;
no weather, no sky,
waxy tube rooted down her throat,
the rest of us bowing
by the high, white bed, praying
for her to drift back down
and later,
for her to rise.

USEFUL THINGS

Julia Tagliere

Be useful, the girl's mother had said before stepping back onto the crowded minibus; the girl's father had not come with them to the station. With each seat already taken, her mother was forced to stand on the bus steps, gripping the bent metal railing. When the bus pulled away, heading back to Dong Van, she had not looked again through the glass at her daughter.

Be useful.

The girl, now closer to a young woman, looked up from the mending desk at the odd, square clock that Auntie said had belonged to the previous tenant of this corner of the strip mall, tucked away on the scruffy edges of this city of twins, named for a Christian saint.

Fifteen minutes, Auntie had told the girl, but the clock's minute hand was missing, so the girl was left to wonder how many minutes remained for her to fill with usefulness. A neatly folded stack of clothes lay at the girl's right hand, a swell of frothy pink peeking out on one side.

Auntie had left little for the girl to do this sluggish Tuesday afternoon: She'd already swept the floor twice; restacked the stand of customers' returned hangers so their unpredictable metal claws all faced the same way; she'd even used the hand iron to press smooth the crumpled wads of damp, pruny bills from the cash drawer. Auntie detested an untidy cash drawer.

"If anyone comes in while I'm gone, get their blue ticket, match it to the number. You won't have to talk, as long as they have the ticket." Auntie showed the girl how to punch the keys on the keyboard that would reveal the customer's item numbers. "Give them their clothes, take their money. Smile. They like that."

But the girl held out little hope for such a diversionary customer, as customers rarely came into Auntie's dry cleaning business on Tuesdays. Auntie had told her it was because they weren't in a hurry, like they were on Saturday afternoons, always trying to beat the Open sign flipping to Closed for Sunday, instead of planning ahead.

Being useful on Saturdays was easy; on Tuesdays, however, the absence of a minute hand mattered less, and on hot summer Tuesdays, it mattered not at all. But be useful, her mother had said, so the girl sat at the mending desk, guessing at the minutes.

She wiped her hands on her smock and picked up the fine, soft item from the top of the stack. When she unfolded it and saw that it was a baby coat, she dropped it, as she would a hissing teapot scalding her fingers. A faint fragrance of tall grass, of baking soil and drying blood, seemed to drift up from the tiny coat, overcoming for an instant the bitterness of Auntie's cleaning fluids. The girl pushed the small garment away, her eyes fixed not on the jacket but on an empty, faraway field.

More minutes passed, somehow more uncountable than the others, except perhaps, by the droplets of sweat beading up on her downy upper lip, before she picked up the garment again to begin the repair.

She smoothed out the lapel and studied the raised pattern embroidered over the very spot where an infant daughter's heart would have warmed the plush cloth. She ran the tip of her finger up and down each delicate curlicue and whorl, circling each arch as one would when tickling the lineless skin on the bottom of a new foot. Never having learned to read, even in her native Hmong dialect, to the girl the stitches there were just a pretty design. They could not signify a name.

On her third attempt to force the needle through the plush fabric, the girl pricked her finger, raising a tiny bead of blood. She sucked at her fingertip and tried not to think of the soft shirt in which she'd wrapped her own daughter before leaving her in the tall grass at the back of the field.

The bell over the door jingled and the girl looked up. She pushed her long bangs back behind her ears and pulled her lips into a wide smile.

"Can I help you?" she said, stuttering out the words Auntie had taught her.

The man who had rung the bell—tall and lopsided with gouged, red cheeks and thick, wire-framed glasses—scanned the store. He placed both hands flat on the desk in front of the girl and the tassel of his knit cap shook. A rapid stream of words rattled out of the man's mouth; the only word the girl caught was 'dress.'

"Ticket?" She twisted the strange word around in her mouth, remembering to keep her lips spread wide in a friendly fashion, like Auntie had told her, but the man's face only grew redder. Why would he wear such a fuzzy hat on such a hot day, she wondered? She glanced at the clock again, but it provided no clue of when her useful minutes would run out.

"Ticket? No ticket," the man said.

He dug at his left ear, and the girl blinked up at the small white tuft of hair sprouting there. He leaned closer to her face and chewed out another chain of sounds, so loudly that the girl felt them drop down onto the desk under her elbows. She heard "dress" again and what sounded, perhaps, like the man's name. He jabbed a squat thumb into his chest and repeated the word three times, louder each time.

"Gunderson. Gunderson. Gunderson."

Inside the stiff new work shoes Auntie had given her when she brought her home from the immigration office, the girl shifted her feet. She blinked up at the man again and repeated, "Ticket," adding "Please" this time. She worked to think of forcing the needle in and out of the soft pink fabric in her hands, trying not to picture her daughter's tiny feet, perfect and bloodied in the tall grass curled around her toes.

"I don't have a ticket." The man was yelling now. He brought his forehead so close to hers that she saw red and purple veins riddling his nose. She breathed in his sour morning coffee and recoiled.

"No ticket?" she asked, shaking her head and trying not to think of the milky scent of her daughter's cheek. Hands trembling, the girl carefully set the plush pink jacket on the desk and tried another smile. "No ticket?" she repeated.

"—English?" Hands bunched into meaty fists, now the man pounded them onto the desk. The girl shook her head back and forth, staring at the man's bubbling lips, trying to pick out a useful word from the torrent spewing forth from them.

She caught "dress" and "stupid," and when he said "bitch" in his loud, angry voice, she rose from the desk and began backing away, shielding her stomach with her useless hands, as her father should have shielded her from her mother's rage. She tried not to think about the stinging in her small, tender breasts, or the dampness she imagined she could still feel spreading across them.

The man snatched the pink jacket from the desk and threw it to the floor. The girl yelped.

"Gunderson. Gunderson." He stepped back and hitched up his shiny, worn trousers, breathing hard.

The girl retreated into the corner, aching for air. She could not take her eyes off the pink jacket, flung so carelessly aside. Because such a thing wasn't useful, she tried not to think of the pinch of her mother's fingers at the bus depot, or the sting of her father's hand across her face when she'd told him of the shame growing in her belly; tried not to think of the blood running down her shaking legs as she'd squatted in the tall grass, or the feeble cries growing fainter against the shirt she had held over her daughter's face. She tried not to think of any of these things, only dug her fists into her soft, empty abdomen and silently pleaded with the clock to show her its missing hand.

"No ticket," she said again, and it was no longer a question, but a confession she wasn't sure the man could hear over the massive fans propped behind the pickup counter; their whirring blades reminded her of the scythes her father and mother used to use to cut the tall grass.

The bell jingling behind the man startled them both and the girl heard Auntie's voice.

"How are you today, sir?" Auntie greeted the man cheerfully. She spotted the plush pink jacket on the floor and glanced coldly at the girl before picking it up. She made a big show of brushing away dirt, although the floor was spotless. She handed the jacket back to the girl and ordered in Hmong, "Get back to work." Auntie took up her post behind the counter again and asked the man, "Picking up?"

"Yes, a dress. Gunderson," the man said loudly. The girl edged along the wall, sat at the desk gingerly, and resumed her work on the broken zipper, trying not to listen. A drop of wetness tickled down the top of her stomach. Sweat, surely; it could no longer be milk. She held the jacket farther away.

The man flung his arm toward the girl and she flinched. In spite of herself, the girl heard more words, useful ones: blue, dress again, three, and two names she recognized as the other dry cleaners in town. Auntie had spat their names on the sidewalk on the girl's first day, then ordered her to clean up the spittle.

"Do you have your ticket?" Auntie spoke briskly over the man's complaints.

"No, I don't have—" the man said.

"Last name?" Auntie asked.

She smiled, and, under the sway of her small, dark eyes, the man began to deflate. He pulled the blue hat from his head, sweat propping up the thinning hair left in its wake. "Gunderson. My wife is—was Theresa."

The girl snuck a peek at Auntie, who was typing something

on the keyboard of the store's computer, a smudged, yellowish box with a permanent rainbow on the screen. Auntie studied the computer screen for a moment, then her face softened, as much as it ever did.

"Mr. Gunderson," Auntie said, and then came two words the girl had already learned by heart. "I'm sorry." Auntie lowered her head for a moment. "She was always very nice. One moment, please, I have her dress." Auntie touched the red button and sent the racks of clothing behind her spinning to life; the plastic bags encasing each garment sighed as they floated past.

Mr. Gunderson settled his weight onto his left leg and hitched up his baggy work pants again without looking at the girl. He watched the clothes glide by; the passing of the racks created a slight breeze that lifted his thinning hair.

Auntie stopped the spinning at precisely the right moment. She plucked a blue dress from the rack, its plastic bag sticky from the heat, and handed it to the man. "No charge," she said.

The girl watched Mr. Gunderson's jowls shake like a rooster's wattle. He said to Auntie, "Thank you. This was her favorite dress," and pressed it tightly to his chest before turning to look at the girl.

She ducked her head, still forcing the needle in and out of the jacket and trying not to think any more useless thoughts about her daughter's tiny body, slippery and warm as it dropped at last from between her shaking legs into her waiting hands, trying not to remember how the tall grass had swallowed the tiny body from view as she'd stumbled back home.

The bell over the door tinkled again as Mr. Gunderson

stepped closer to the mending desk, letting through the door he held open a blast of dense, greasy air from outside. The girl kept her eyes on his shoes, which did not match. Because Auntie had not told her anything, the girl did not know what to do.

"I'm sorry," he said to the girl. She did not lift her eyes. "Thank you."

The door shut behind him, the bell jingling merrily.

After a moment, Auntie placed a hand on the girl's shoulder and spoke to her in their Hmong dialect. "His wife died this week; I made a note in the computer. This is why you must learn."

The girl carefully tied off the pink thread and snipped it in two with Auntie's sewing shears.

"Yes, Auntie," she said. She slid the zipper smoothly open and shut and thought of an empty field, of the need for useful things, and of Auntie's hand, hard on her shoulder.

TIRESIAS

LUCIEN DARJEUN MEADOWS

Standing on the corner of High and Jackson
    Beside the boarded-up bus stop at 1 a.m.,
His face and hands stained familiar coaldark
    But his hair pure white, and his eyes a blue
That shocks you back to the first boy you loved
    In fourth grade, before you were pulled from school
For your own good, a blue you imagine water could be
    Somewhere, not here. He sees you looking, hums
His own country song: *Wife left me, took our kids,*
    Even took the dog. Starts naming his father's fathers,
        The counties they first homesteaded in, like you,
Started up in Buckhannon, down to Jackson and Roane,
    And you wait for the words you can predict
        In his squint and limp, just like your grandfathers—

By the rust-peach sunrise, you two are down
    Swinging your feet beside the Monongahela shore,
And he weaves you into deep narrow tunnels
    Under mountains, the dry cough of headlamps
And wet cough inevitable after a couple years,
    The constant stench of each cave waiting
For an excuse to burn, the grey bathwater

And laundry tubs, and the unnatural white
Of the county inspector's cuffs. The man
    Shakes off his denim jacket, unbuttons his shirt,
        Shows you the purple and grey blotches running
Down his right side from collarbone to hipbone,
    Says *When that mine started to buckle, I thought*—
    And you both watch the river for a minute—

Lost my best buddy that day, worked together
    Almost two decades. And you wonder if
That friend could be your father, since the date
    Is about right. Then he asks if you believe
The dead are all watching, waiting for revenge
    On those who slipped by, and you feel
The cool dark voice you sometimes hear
    When you lie at the bottom of the Kanawha
And let yourself think *This is the way*
    A world could end until your body, your canary,
        Pushes you up to the surface, choking, like now,
Surrounded by ghosts you want to declare
    Absurd, but you both hear the wind, the tide,
        Your father's blood in your veins, saying *I believe.*

THE WOODEATERS

Melanie Henderson

There is a river,
just barely a river,
named after a legume,
tamarind.

Its coasts are lined
with deep brown women
wearing lush green afros,
termite mounds adorn their hair
like quartz broaches.

Inside the muddy mounds, a mother
has carved out a new womb
with her beak; a parrot,
hooded, orange or blue,
will emerge with no clue
of what great balance or symbiosis,
has made possible its formation,
its flight. Pure magic:
the woodeaters will cover
a predator in seconds flat; all
else but the mother and the egg.

10 degrees from the center,
the women surrender to the sun,
dip their slender roots in low water.

This magic,
wet and mysterious,
hangs over the river,
just barely a river,
named after a legume,
tamarind.

HOW TO KEEP GOING

Melanie Henderson

Unwatered lips touch the baby's face.

You admire the way she dives into a field of purple flowers,
arms opened as wide as her ginger eyes.

If you dive your large bones into the mess of lavender,
they will surely break; underneath the brush, there is soil
as hard as half-dried cement to discourage your frolicking.

She is giggling and rolling her softness
over the blue-violet spikes as if they were thick,
white clouds losing not one speck of joy to the promise of bruises.

Plump, clumsy, fearless, she mashes pudgy fingers into calices,
    rubs her nose in the calm of mauve, snatches up
    a bouquet and offers it to the sky.

The *vert* stems break many times, in many places.
    —not one fist of petals is raised in defense
    against her small weight.

There are only whorls of surrender,
and dye in her palms.

TAKING IT

SUE EISENFELD

I had been in awe for years of the clever mind behind the septic company's motto: "You make it, we take it," printed on a sign outside a low-slung building near a small, rural Virginia village. And so when it came time to inspect the septic system and pump the septic tank at our remote country cabin at the foot of a mountain—never done in the whole 40-year history of the place—I knew immediately who I'd call.

We had arranged the date and time weeks before over the phone, and I drove out there, a few hours from home, where split-rail fence zigzags modern art over rolling wheat-colored foothills. I made special arrangements to take off work and spend the night so I'd be there on a Monday morning. The cabin landline didn't work when I got there—it went out every once in a while due to rain or wind—but everything had been made clear in advance, even how payment would work, as I mentioned to the guy that my husband Neil and I were the caretakers of the cabin, not the owners. Rick had made some assumptions about the owner by saying, "Rich people never pay on time." I had put that statement away and moved on.

I was standing on the stoop outside the screen door in greeting when the truck arrived, right on time as far as I was concerned—8:30 a.m. So when Rick jumped out of the vehicle and started yelling at me immediately—about how he'd been driving around for more than an hour, how he had called me eight times and had gotten a busy signal, how he even stopped into a county building looking for any record of my residence, how I had given him the wrong address, and basically informed me that I was a common asshole—I received the onslaught straight on. He was a fat-fingered, stocky fellow, maybe early 50s, with two much-younger workers, and he had his hissy fit on the trampled front lawn in full view of a glorious long-distance Appalachian mountain landscape and then turned his back to me without even a single Southern-gentleman hello.

He'd only found us at all because Neil had just left for work and had seen the truck driving up and down our dirt road and had directed the guy up our half-mile driveway. My heart was racing, and I swore I would never, ever, ever have a contractor (usually men) come to this place without Neil around again. I turned my back to him as well and tore into the house where I paced for half an hour, sweating, trying to pull myself together, knowing full well I had told him "two twenty" not "two ten" and that after two and a half years of being a full-time renter (in an experiment in slower-paced rural living) before becoming the caretaker under a different owner, I knew my own goddamned address.

Let me step back a minute off my country-living high horse, to explain that this Northern-city-girl-who-grew-up-in-a-high-rise-apartment-building turned metropolitan-Mid-Atlantic-suburbanite didn't even know what a septic tank or septic system was most of my life; waste just "went away." In college, I learned that in metropolitan areas waste is piped from residences and processed chemically in a treatment plant, and then, once cleaned, released into a river. I'd actually taken tours of this type of municipal sewage treatment plant as part of an environmental policy course and had visited plants in various cities around the country in which I was interviewing mayors for a job in environmental communications.

Neil had introduced me to this new world of more primitive disposal for less-developed areas because the nature center he operates in a rural location uses a septic system as well, and he's the de facto manager of it. There, waste is piped out of buildings to an underground tank to begin breaking down and then distributed into a drain field with perforated pipes to be absorbed and filtered into the soil. I had been around for the period of time when the nature center was transitioning from wooden outhouses (where waste goes straight from the cut-out hole of a toilet seat you're sitting on to the deep cavity in the ground into which it falls) to real bathrooms and this more refined and civilized process of handling these natural functions. I had been aware of the siting of the septic field higher up on a mountain than the drinking-water well below it, which never seemed right. And I had always scoffed at naming the septic field after the founder of the nature center, who had scouted out more than two hundred acres of undeveloped country wilderness for suburban schoolchildren to enjoy, because that "honor" always seemed misplaced: *We named a field full of shit after you, thank you very much.*

But back to the country cabin: I knew the mistake was on his end, though since I was about to endure an hour or more with three strong, strange men (although the two young men were very polite, calling me "ma'am" and all), I eventually swallowed my righteous angst and went back out there and put on my smiley face and sweetest tongue and apologized for any "miscommunication." He accepted my apology and simply told me it was "frustrating." Then he went on to poke around the ground with a metal rod trying to find the septic tank and all its components—the septic line, the distribution box, and the septic field, as no one knew where they were.

As Murphy's Law would have it, the place where I had decided to park my new, shiny red, mid-life-crisis sporty car—in the farthest back place of the gravel parking area away from the house, to allow the truck the most room to maneuver and turn around at the awkward top of our winding driveway—was the site of the septic tank. Not in the open area at the bottom of the cabin's front steps, where I was so convinced the tank was located that I stopped parking my car there for fear the tank might be rusted out and my car would sink into the ground. So now, after moving my car slightly out of the way upon his command, my new baby was wedged between the giant truck that sucks out the poop and all the machinery and equipment the boys had hauled up there to find the tank, dig out its top, and pry it open to look inside. Rick told me, "You're lucky your car didn't fall in."

The septic line, as it turned out, was sagging and located under standing water, whereas it was supposed to be straight and flat and above the water level underground. Because fixing that would cost thousands of dollars, and the place was now owned by a nonprofit organization, I asked what the risk was of doing nothing.

The line could back up, he said, and shit would start coming out the outlet pipe in the front lawn. The situation would not be a problem if it were just Neil and me living there, but the fact that the place was rented out to various strangers from the Washington, DC area each weekend of the year made it risky. "You never know what city people might put in there," he said with a sneer, referring to baby wipes and other inappropriate matter that people flush down.

I tried to recover from this affront to my native people by asking what had happened to his clever sign and motto, as I had driven past his place the day before and it was gone. He thanked me very much for my compliment and explained how the sign was larger than county rules allowed, and so he had to take it down. And then we talked about the size of the septic tank and how he might write out his inspection report in such a way as to make clear how the owner could rectify the problem and he could get the business. And then I brought out my Tupperware of homemade browned-butter brownies I had baked recently and was hoping to foist off on someone else so I wouldn't be tempted, and the two boys put their sewage-water-covered hands in there and took one while Rick, who maybe wondered about losing a few pounds himself, abstained and laughed at my reason for giving them away.

And by the end I think we had a meeting of the minds and a cordial engagement. He didn't know where I was from or what kind of person I was.

As he drove away, I felt pretty proud of myself for diffusing a fraught situation on my own, on the eve of the first night I would spend by myself at the cabin—the only person on 40 acres and no other neighbors in sight or earshot. Sometime that holy night of Milky Way sky dew and mooing cows echoing throughout the hollows, it finally dawned on me that it could have been my lingering Philadelphia accent that had caused him to mishear me on the address: "two twunny" or "two twenny" could have come out sounding like "two ten," possibly, if I swallowed my last syllable. But maybe I am trying too hard to cross a divide larger than linguistic, between the two worlds I inhabit and embrace but that may be too far away from one another ever to bridge.

EVEN IN THE JUNK YARD

Raymond Philip Asaph

where the chained dog climbs the air
as the headlights of rusting school bus stare,
miracles, or at least good deals,
are possible. And though the grease on the dirt
seems permanent—and lethal—
dandelions nevertheless rise from this soil,
their delicate heads shredding in the oily wind
beside the warped wooden steps of the shack.
Inside, under a cracked black clock,
the junk man, eating a meatball hero,
wipes his beard with the back of his hand,
smiles as he stands and becomes—somehow—
a gentleman in a stained gray shirt
when the woman with the bright white skirt walks in.

DRIVING IN IOWA, EAST ON HIGHWAY 30

Samantha Leigh Futhey

Outside of towns, men chop the dead
grass on riding mowers. Blocks
of square houses lean against

splinters of corn stubble. A train
clips across fields, hauling oil
through the country's girth,

not pausing in its urgency.
Charlie's Gun Shop, cemeteries,
roads of dust marked by truck tires,

stream banks cleaved raw
with mud, wind turbines
stirring air for energy—

all passed with little
remorse. Lopsided in a yard,
a trailer sags, *For Sale*

scrawled on its shell.
Outsiders, we can't discern
what's for sale: trailer, caved-in

house yawning to sky,
piles of bent cars, all the land
rolled out like a sheet

of dough tired of constant
kneading. You talk of buying
a house shaded by mountains,

pine-embraced, leaving
this flat country, pressing
forward from the lost

glamour of corn, small
town pride, wide open
faces you fly by without

a second glance. I look
at those silvered hills, split
between what's harvested

and what's left for reaping,
apprehensive of the next turn.

FARMALL

Samantha Leigh Futhey

My father, arms and legs smeared
oil black, ripped jeans and shirt
hay-dusted, cranks wrenches
in the tractor's rusted gut to repair

what he thinks he can
fix with force.

I pass him tools, the unfamiliar
weight settling in his hands
to cure vibrations of a faulty
engine, attempts to rewire,

start again. I count seconds
to meltdown because here's how

every repair ends: the tractor's bulk
shudders at his smacks, the barrels
that held him burst, oozing. A man
taught to bust and crumple,

a practitioner of eruption,
his father's pupil. As his witness,

I stand back, grip my elbows. I can't look
at my hands, so clean, so empty.

COMPANY

MARY GRIMM

Grace tapped her fingers against the ashtray sitting next to her on the couch. Before her wedding six months ago, people had given her things like a pewter coffee set, and delicate footed mugs with matching plates—the kind of thing that her mother and the other older women who had chosen them expected she would use when people came visiting. She imagined that they had thought of her pouring coffee from the pewter coffee pot and cutting homemade cake to put on the flowered plates.

"Do you want another hit?" Jimmy asked her.

"Mmhmm," she said. He had come over to hang out with Sean, who wasn't here. He had hardly seemed to listen when she explained that Sean was at the park three blocks away, playing basketball with some guys he knew from high school. Jimmy's eyes were glassy and wide. He was high, she knew, but it didn't bother her. Jimmy was always cool. He never got weird or crazy.

They were sitting on the ancient sectional sofa she had gotten at a garage sale. Some time long ago in the past it must have been in fashion, although it was hard to believe that anyone had ever wanted a brown upholstered monster with scratchy gold threads in a maddening pattern. Jimmy was sprawled at one end and she sat at the other, her legs drawn up, her chin resting on her knees. He leaned forward to pass her the joint they were sharing.

"Sean is..." he paused while she inhaled, but then didn't go on.

"Playing basketball?" she said, holding her breath and the smoke in. Her words squeaked out. In a few minutes she would find that unbearably funny, but now she felt embarrassed.

"Basketball," Jimmy said. "He always liked that kind of thing."

"I can give him a message," Grace said. "If he doesn't come back."

He looked at her gravely, and she felt as if what she'd said had some kind of importance that she didn't realize. "I thought we'd all go the Picadilly," Jimmy said slowly. She'd passed the joint back to him and he held it consideringly between thumb and finger. "I'm going to roadie for Dragonwyck, and I can bring along anyone I want." He inhaled, held it, then let the smoke trickle out. "For free," he added. He leaned forward to pass the joint back, and rested one hand on her leg, balancing.

The touch of his hand was surprising to her. She looked down at it, darker than her very fair skin. She could never get a tan, no matter how she tried. Her mother said it was just as well, since tanning made for wrinkles, but her legs looked sick in summer, white, like the underside of a fish. She took the joint and pushed at Jimmy so that he moved back.

"You ever been there?" he asked.

"Where?" she said.

"The Picadilly."

"No. Is it nice?"

"It's a dive." He laughed. "That's why we love it."

Who was we, she wondered.

He leaned forward, and she tensed, thinking he would touch her again. "You going to take a hit or what?"

Grace had forgotten about the joint. She barely sipped at it, for she could feel the cloudy heaviness beginning to fill her head, and passed it back. It was so short now that his fingers were close to its burning end. He pinched it knowingly and inhaled, his teeth showing.

She wished that Sean would come back, although she was mad at him. He hadn't wanted to go to the mall with her, or to the coffee house, or to the park, or in fact anywhere at all with her. Do you think you're still in high school, she'd yelled at him. Because you're not. You're a married man. She didn't like to think of the ugly look that had come over his face when she said that, as if he hated the sound of it. It's not as if I like being married all that much, she thought now. The beginning part was fun, the sex, and sleeping in the same bed. But the rest. She rubbed the bare soles of her feet against the scratchy couch, which seemed to wake nerves in her body she hadn't known about. Jimmy had laid his head against the back of the couch and was staring at the ceiling.

"Let's go outside," Jimmy said.

"It's getting dark," she said.

"No, no," he said, shaking his head. He got up, barely stumbling. "This high needs room to expand. We have to be outside for this one."

"Why?" she said, but he didn't answer, and when he held

out his hand, she took it. He pulled her to her feet in a smooth move that made her feel as if she had thinned and lightened, as if her bones were filling with air.

They went through the house without turning on the lights, and out the back door. The uncut grass brushed against her ankles and made her itch, but the itch seemed wonderful, a luscious abrasion that made her skin start to burn. The backyard was darker than the street and she and Jimmy melted into the shadows. There were two lawn chairs, one overturned, but Jimmy passed them and led her to the square of grass that was bounded by the chainlink fence and two garages, one belonging to the old woman next door. The grass here was even longer, and when Jimmy sank down into it, pulling her with him, it brushed against her ankles. Jimmy let go of her hand. She had felt silly and childish when he was pulling her across the yard, but now she felt untethered, as if her lightness would become a serious liability. If there were a wind, she might blow along the ground, she thought, like a plastic bag from the grocery store belled out into a sail.

Jimmy stubbed the joint they'd finished into the dirt, scraping back the grass to make a place for it. He tore off grass and dandelion leaves and laid them over the joint. "In nomine patri, ..." He lit another joint he pulled from his shirt pocket and handed it to her. "I used to be an altar boy," he said. When Grace took it and put it between her lips, he said, "This is my body, this is my blood."

"That's perverted," she said, and took a good long drag. Out here in the near dark, she felt better than she had in the house, but she was glad that they were back by the garage, more or less out of sight. The old woman who lived next door was always spying. She kept coming over and bringing cookies, but she never stopped looking around when she was in the house, snooping. She asked questions about how often Grace did the dishes, and if she waxed the floor or only mopped.

"I'll never wax a floor," she said to Jimmy. "I won't do it."

"That's cool," he said. "So, do you want to go?"

"Go where?" She could see the old woman's kitchen window from here, a yellow square of light. The old woman crossed the square, carrying something. A plate with something on it. Maybe cake. Maybe she had company. We both have company, she thought, which was funny. It was very funny, really.

"The Picadilly."

"Sean's not back yet." She watched the old woman cross back and forth, carrying things that she couldn't quite see.

"If you come, you can meet Jojo. He's the lead singer."

"I know," she said, although she had no idea who he was.

"All the girls like him."

"I know, I know."

"He's got charisma, which is a pretty cool word, don't you think?"

She crossed her legs and sat up primly. "I don't like him." Her head felt remarkably steady, its balance on her shoulders something to be admired.

"You don't?" Jimmy rolled over on his side, as if he wanted to see her face.

"I don't like him at all."

"Who do you like?" His voice was very quiet. There was no wind and his voice was a small thing in the dark air.

She looked at him, squinting a little. "This is silly," she said.

"Not as silly as some things," Jimmy said. "Some things are so silly I can't hardly stand it. Like politics. If you want to talk about silly." He moved a little nearer.

The joint was burning in her fingers, and she took an absentminded drag. Jimmy's hair fell over the arm he had his head propped on, so long that it trailed in the grass, or probably did. It was too dark to be sure.

"Girls are silly sometimes," he said. "Not you though—you're pretty straight."

"The dog next door is silly," Grace said. "My neighbor's dog. He's, you know, a poodle," she made circles in the air with her hands, "all poofy and curly." She began to laugh, and Jimmy laughed, too. "He wears a bow." She put her hands over her mouth.

Jimmy laughed again. "What color?"

"Sssh," she said, "don't laugh." But she couldn't stop either.

"What color?" he said, moving closer.

"Stop, it's too funny," she said. They both laughed harder, taking gasping breaths, trying to stifle themselves. She firmed up her mouth and took a deep breath, held up one hand as if to say, wait. "Ok," she said, her laughter under control. "We have to be quiet. I mean it." She looked toward the neighbor's house. There were two people in the kitchen now, her neighbor and another old woman, arranged in the window looking toward each other as if they were in a painting. Their mouths were moving, but she couldn't tell if they were talking or chewing. This almost made her start laughing again, but she bit her lip so she wouldn't.

"Math is silly. No, it's stupid," Jimmy said. "School is stupid. I'm glad to be out of all that."

She nodded, although she had liked school, mostly. "Housework is stupid," she said.

"Doing dishes is the stupidest thing in the world. You have to do them every day."

Jimmy nodded at this truth. "Do you have any cookies? Like Oreos?"

"I don't know," she said. "I could go and look."

"No, don't go. It's no big."

The grass was warm and slightly damp. It was black now, all the color drained out of the shadows between the garages. The joint was done, and Jimmy buried it next to the first one, drifting bits of weed over it with ceremonial care.

"Sean should be back soon," she said, although probably he wouldn't be. He always went to the Jigsaw for a beer after.

"Soon," Jimmy said, drawing the word out, "Soooooon. If we were out in the country, we'd be able to see the stars."

"I suppose," she said.

"The stars aren't stupid," Jimmy said.

"No," she said.

"They aren't," he insisted, as if she had disagreed. He had moved a little, turning his face to the light from her neighbor's window. Grace could see the bridge of his nose, and the high curve of his cheekbone. "You know what's totally stupid?" he said.

"What?" She didn't care really, but she was starting to feel odd, as if she had separated from herself, as if one part of her had drawn away and was looking at the other part with cold dislike.

Jimmy's head darted forward, and though the motion was quick, it seemed to take a long time, his hair falling forward, the little rustle of the grass as his body moved over it. She jerked back, thinking he was going to take her arm, but instead he licked her knee, his tongue rough and warm. He lapped at it slowly, and she saw the glitter of his eye, watching her while he did it.

He lay back again, his eyes still on her. "Basketball," he said. "Basketball is the stupidest thing on earth."

Grace pulled both knees against her chest reflexively, circling them with her arms. Now she ought to get up, or invoke Sean's name. "I'm a married woman," she said, but this sounded so ridiculous that it made her laugh. She had a vision of herself in an old-fashioned dress saying this to someone holding a gun—something she'd seen in a movie, she realized, and thought herself very clever to have pinned this down.

"Marriage is stupid," Jimmy said.

Grace sighed. She hugged her knees more tightly. "It is, kind of. But I still am."

"Your call," Jimmy said. He lay back down on the grass, his arms crossed behind his head. "The question is, should we or shouldn't we."

Grace squinted at him, trying to make out his face in the near dark. "I already said."

"I meant, roll another joint." He patted his shirt pocket.

"I've got enough for one more."

Grace looked over at the next door window. Her neighbor was pouring something from a green teapot into a matching cup that her guest held out to her. She felt a space inside herself that she hadn't noticed before, a space that Jimmy had somehow shown her. "I don't care," she said.

"Should I or shouldn't I waste a perfectly good jay on someone who doesn't care." Jimmy was holding out a bag of weed on the palm of his hand as if he were balancing it on scales.

Grace would have liked to get up and walk away, but her knees and in fact all her joints felt disconnected. It would be embarrassing to fall, to have Jimmy see her fall and try to get up. She'd always been clumsy, as her mother had often pointed out to her. She could hear her mother's voice saying it—you've always been clumsy, and you should have known better than to smoke that awful stuff.

"I'm going to take that as a yes." Jimmy deftly rolled the cigarette paper into a neat tube, tucked in at both ends. "I say we should smoke this and then..." he let his voice trail off.

"Then what?" Grace asked. She could hear the phone ringing inside the house, her phone, her house. Who would it be? Her mother. Sean, saying he was bringing back some pizza. Ginny who maybe wanted to come over and hang out. It might be good if Ginny came over, because she could talk to Jimmy, and to Grace's mother if she showed up. Sean would not be coming with pizza. He was at the Jigsaw right now with a beer in front of him watching one of his stupid friends pretend he knew how to play pool.

"Then you can decide whether you want to blow me or not," Jimmy said. He handed her the joint. "Just kidding."

"Where did you meet Sean?" Grace took the joint. Her lips were wet and the paper stuck when she drew in.

"Sean and my brother went to high school together. They were on the football team." He shot her with his finger. "Football is stupid. You know that, right?"

"I don't know," Grace said. "I don't know anything."

"Listen to me then," Jimmy said. He sat up and put his face close to hers. "Listen to me, and I'll tell you. Whatever you want to know."

"I don't know what I want to know," Grace said.

"Neither do I," Jimmy said. "That's what makes it so perfect." He leaned in, and she watched his features grow sharper. His eyes had a wet shine, his mouth looked soft, half hidden in the careless growth of his beard. His hair was longer than hers, which would make her mother frown in distaste. It fell forward as he moved against her and she could feel it touching her arms where they were bare below the short sleeves of her blouse.

Jimmy put his mouth on hers, rubbing it as if he was asking a question. As if she were a lamp, Grace thought, and he was Aladdin. How stupid she was, to be thinking of such a thing. Why couldn't she be thinking of something romantic, why couldn't she be a princess or an actress. Why couldn't there be a candle or—- she didn't know, but—

"Kiss me for real," Jimmy said. "Do I have to do all the work?"

Grace put a hand up and found his hair. She took a handful

and pulled it, but didn't move her mouth away. They were both leaning forward, their bodies otherwise untouching. "Maybe I don't want to kiss you," she said, but she didn't move away.

Jimmy put his fingers on her lips and pulled at the lower one a little. "Come on, Gracie. Come on."

"Kissing is stupid," Grace said. She opened her mouth a little, and he sucked on her tongue.

"No, it isn't." Jimmy's voice was muffled, his mouth moving on hers, burrowing inside.

Grace's eyes were open—it seemed wrong to close them and abandon herself to this entirely. She could see the side of her neighbor's garage past Jimmy's shoulder, dark with a slash of light from the streetlight that revealed the peeling paint in harsh relief. Her neighbor had a car but she never drove it. It had belonged to her husband, who was dead. She didn't know how to drive. How could she stand not knowing how to drive? Her son would come once a week and drive her in the car to grocery shop. What kind of a life was that?

Jimmy reached forward and put his hands on her shoulders, pulling her toward and under him a little, and Grace let herself be moved. His flannel shirt was unbuttoned, and she could feel his skin against hers above the neck of her blouse. He took his mouth away from hers for a minute. "Jesus, Grace," he said. He nuzzled against her neck, pushing inside her collar. He held her shoulder with one hand, and with the other began to pull at the waistband of her shorts.

Grace let her head fall back. She was thinking about Sean, how she'd met him at Ginny's. He had looked at her from across Ginny's basement for a long time before he came over. Jimmy's hand was fumbling at the buttons of her blouse and she wiggled a little in a way that might have meant she wanted him to get off, but she knew it didn't mean that at all. Jimmy slid his hand into her half unbuttoned blouse and panted against her neck. "What about the Picadilly," Grace said, her mouth against his ear.

"The Picadilly is stupid," Jimmy said.

"Wait," Grace said. "I mean it."

Jimmy stopped moving. He lay half across her, one hand in her blouse, the other underneath her, almost inside her shorts. "Grace," he said. "Gracie Grace."

"I don't want to—" Grace said, but he interrupted her, moving his mouth against the skin of her chest.

"You don't want to go to the Picadilly," he said. "I'm telling you that so you'll know it."

Grace's shoulders twitched. She felt as if she were sinking into the grass. She could feel its dampness working its way into her clothes. "What if I do want to go?"

Jimmy rolled away from her but kept his hands on her. "You don't. You know what goes on in the johns there?" He rubbed back and forth with just the tips of his fingers. "People getting it on every which way. Scoring drugs. There's something else for you to know."

Grace didn't answer. The sky was not black but a very dark blue, something she wouldn't have guessed. It was a color that had to be experienced to be known. "Would you like some coffee?" she asked.

"Coffee is stupid," Jimmy said. He bent over and pushed

his mouth onto hers, and when she tried weakly to slide out from under him, he clamped her arms and held her down.

He only half undressed her, unbuttoned her blouse the rest of the way and pulled her shorts and underwear down, and she let him, lifting her hips to help. All the while, and while he was pushing inside her, she kept her eyes open, watching the sky, and her neighbor's window, which shone yellow like a rectangular sun. Her neighbor's company was gone. Soon she would go to bed, for she didn't stay up much past ten. Soon, Grace said to herself. Soon Sean would come home, or he wouldn't.

THE EGG

Richard Jones

Will I ever shape a poem or work of art more mysterious than the egg—the pure white of the shell? —the simple oval shape?—the inscrutable world inside? Heavy in the palm, its weight delights the hand. A hundred years ago my grandfather, a blacksmith, sold eggs as a side business. He raised chickens in three henhouses. Because I once asked, my mother wrote a little essay for me called "Chickens." She wrote of how she'd ride in the truck with my grandfather to the train station. The Southern Line brought wooden crates packed with chicks— thousands of tiny biddies. She wrote about going into the dark of the hen houses to collect the eggs, sorting them by size— small, medium, and large—and placing them in baskets to sell. Eggs helped the family survive the Depression. The world was changing and the blacksmith's days were numbered, but my grandfather would not be defeated. He worked at his forge until the day he died. My mother wrote her memories for me in blue ink in longhand when she was almost ninety, her cursive script flowing across the white page, elegant and lovely, like rolling waves of time. Maybe I inherited my love of mystery from my mother, and the fire and iron—the strength and resolve to stay at it—from my grandfather.

BLUE STARS

Richard Jones

Yesterday I made a to-do list,
a dozen tasks I would undertake
and check off the list one-by-one.
But what did I do with my list?
Did I put it on the piano?
Did I set it down by the coffee pot?
I remember this morning
in my robe at the back door
contemplating frost icing the grass
and seeing a dark-eyed junco at the bird feeder.
How did I know it was a junco
and not a sparrow?
Maybe juncos and sparrows are cousins.
I thought about birds in nests
of twigs, reeds, briars, and straw.
The clear cold sky brought the image
of my late father, high up
and far away, flying
once again in his silver plane,
and I closed my eyes to admire
the many blue paintings
hanging in the gallery of my childhood heart.

Perhaps at that moment
I had the to-do list in my hand
and during my azure reverie
the paper slipped from my fingers.
I only know that when I opened my eyes
I saw it would be wise
to give my blue paintings away—
only then would my heart be free
to help those in need.
I resolved to put that on my to-do list
and that's when I noticed
my to-do list had vanished.
Now the frost has died,
the sun is pushing noon,
and I'm still in my robe
with eternity hovering in the balance.
But no day is without its victory.
Wherever it is hiding,
I'll search for the lost little piece of paper
and when I find it
I'll write down my heart's resolution.
Then I'll dress for the day and go out into the world
and with my pen and to-do list in hand,
I'll draw little blue stars
beside all the accomplished tasks—
buying milk,
picking up the laundry,
driving to the library
and paying the fines for my overdue books.

THE SUITCASE

RICHARD JONES

When I was five I told myself:
if you're going to go to sleep,
you'd better pack a suitcase,
because there's no promise
the world will be here
when you get back.
Your father will be gone—
he'll fly away like a bird.
And your mother
will be in a distant hospital,
dying, or dead,
and you will never see her
or your father ever again.
The house you live in
and the room you love
will vanish like any dream
and you will find yourself
lost at sea, shipwrecked,
marooned on some green island.
But at least you will have your belongings,
all carefully packed in your suitcase—
your loyal teddy bear
and silver spoon,
your cowboy hat and six shooters.

THE GIRLS WITH THE ISSUE OF BLOOD

Afua Ansong

Instead of blood, we crushed grapes into our underwear to show our mothers the color of purity: It wasn't a miracle Jesus would perform so we prayed each pumpkin night that maybe our men wouldn't rape us, maybe our skins wouldn't itch like yam leaves when they looked beyond our eyes and felt themselves drop seedlings in our earth. We returned to the crowd, humming a song for a savior. We cried *we're dirty, unholy* and stretched our sea filled arms to stain the hem of his garment.

WOMAN: BECOMING

Afua Ansong

In this scene of the movie, the woman calls her boyfriend
30 times. It is enough
for her to know he does wild
things but she needs proof
so she goes to his house and
asks why he hasn't picked
her 30 phone calls not why
he would cheat. The man is not

overwhelmed but hopes she'll leave
but the eyes of a doubting
woman are sharp: She sees.
A rubber. She starts with rage,
she must touch evidence.
He refuses to fall: un
-dress his disgrace. She is not
satisfied the least, a woman in distress
is not satisfied by a boy's anger.

So in this scene, she picks
a bottle with every ounce of heart
break left in her. She seeks a discovery:
a pulse to the boy she kissed
and told she was a virgin.

EMBARGOES

Matthew Socia

Nancy Edwards rearranged the hats near her millinery's window. The best trimmed hats should be near the window, shouldn't they, where the ladies walking Back Street would see them and then wander themselves in for a buy. But no one would buy. There wasn't enough money to buy. The embargo was still eating at Boston's edges. A ten minute walk from her millinery—named, stupidly, "Miss Edwards" by her brother, Benjamin—were the wharves where the invalid ships bobbed like rotten buoys. It was 1809, February, near the end of a winter of above average snowfall. Nancy liked that some of her customers blamed the snowfall on the embargo. Wouldn't they blame the embargo as well if they were still wearing their summer hats straight through Christmas? She liked when they blamed her hat selection on the embargo, but there was likely truth in that. She liked to get them going on the embargo or the president. If they were chatty, they might buy, but no one was buying hats. She could sometimes sell a simple ground: the basic, untrimmed version of a hat which in better times would leave her store fancily adorned. The embargo had enlightened Boston's women on the beauty of sleek minimalism. She herself didn't wear a hat at work—she kept her blond hair long and loose so she could show the women all the different ways to put on her hats. Now she mostly sold pins and buttons. Gloves, of course, for the wretched snow sent to New England by President Jefferson. Sometimes Nancy sold an exotic-looking bird feather, which she would sew onto an old hat as a frugal re-upholstery. *I didn't even make the ground,* she would think as the feather bounced out her door.

She looked at her inventory. She had excess hats dangling on their stands like dead birds from another world. At least she could make another world with her hats: with the embargo, there was only Boston things to look at. Until the boats stopped toddling in, she hadn't realized how much she liked the movement of goods through a city. Fish, fruit, nuts, meat, silk, plush, fleece. Every day Boston was scraped anew and filled with more stuff. A trimmed hat with a bright ground, feathers curling asymmetrical over the brim—it was a taste of something foreign.

Noon arrived, no customers. Nancy closed Miss Edwards for a minute to buy venison and potatoes for Benjamin. He was ill. Yesterday, she had made him a chicken pie, and he'd liked it. After closing for the day, she would make him a new pie.

When she returned, there was a squat, frog-shaped woman waiting at the door with a red-headed girl, about ten, grinding her shoe into the cobblestone outside the shop.

"We've been waiting. And you're not wearing a hat," the woman said as Nancy unlocked the shop. "A milliner not wearing a hat in this weather?"

Upon entering, Nancy was happy to see the new arrangement

of trimmed hats she'd spent the morning on. She knew she was getting better at millinery. She knew she was right to have pressured her brother into helping her start her enterprise. She showed the woman around, talking about the hats she'd made, the materials, the shapes, and, hoping something would stick, the snow, the embargo, and President Jefferson. But the woman wanted to talk about only craft. "How do you attach a feather?" she asked.

Nancy showed her the stitch she used. They practiced together on a piece of muslin while the girl pulled bits of ribbon from their shelves. Nancy would have to redo the folding later.

"And this pompom? How do you make it? How do you keep it on?"

Nancy showed her, and showed her, too, when the woman asked how to mold a frame, how to attach the ground, and how to secure millinery suppliers.

"My, you're interested. Are you starting your own shop to bankrupt me?" Nancy asked.

"Well, I don't know about bankrupt, but yes," the woman said. "My husband has an extra lot on Prince Street and said I could do what I will with it, so here I am, and I think I've decided. Don't you think I'd be good at making hats? I've passed by your shop a lot and admired it. Don't take offense, but the millinery I use is out toward Cambridge. A family friend. I'd come here if I could, of course."

Prince Street was the very next street. This woman would drive her out. "Friends are friends," Nancy said. "I can't be offended about a thing like that."

"Do you think," the woman said, "that you could teach me

some of the trade? I'd love to surprise my friend by simply one day having my own millinery, full form. She'd die, don't you think? I assure you I'll learn fast. My father used to teach at Harvard."

When Nancy was young, she had imagined running her own millinery the way some girls imagine their weddings. She had turned her tiny room into a pretend shop, with doll-sized hats made of remnants of discarded clothing, which she would sell and resell to her and her brothers' dolls. She had grown up after the war, accompanying America in childhood, a fledgling country of freedom and enterprise, where a young girl's make-believe millinery could one day become real. She could not give up her shop to this woman—she would do anything to keep Miss Edwards afloat.

"My brother is ill, you see," Nancy said. She began to reorganize the mess the girl had made. "I'm taking care of him. And there's this terrible embargo going on." She gripped a bit of orange satin very hard with both her hands, and put it back with deep wrinkles. "Perhaps if times were different, I could help you."

The woman watched her awhile, then said, "Of course, of course. This president is ruining us all. I shouldn't rely on someone to guide me, anyway. Katie, let's buy you a hat as thanks for her helping us."

Nancy sold them a green felt hood with an orange tassel, the cheapest hat they could buy. *But at least it was a hat,* Nancy thought. *At least I sold them a hat before they ruin me.*

They left, shuffling into the slushy street. Nancy stared at the work station of her millinery. Why had she been so cruel as to shut this woman out? They would both be out of business soon—better to sink with a comrade than with an enemy. Nancy took a turban off its stand, her highest priced hat at sixty-five cents, in cream-colored silk. She had trimmed it over a year past. No one would buy the thing, so she tossed it to the ground by the door, but the moment it landed, her heart leapt at her rashness, and she picked it up with pincered fingers as she would a soiled washrag.

There was now a tiny spot of dirt on the turban. She set to work washing it, cursing herself at her stupidity. The spot came off easily, and as she was resetting the turban on its stand, another woman came in—two in an afternoon! Hatless, the woman's hair was stretched tight into a braided bun: the perfect beauty work of a hired servant. Her eyes were red and moist from, Nancy assumed, the rushing winter cold.

The woman set about rummaging through Nancy's hats. "Is this all you have?" she asked.

"This is what I have trimmed and ready. But I can make anything to order. Tell me your style, and I'll make you a hat."

"Well, I need a funeral hat for tomorrow morning," she said. "And none of these will do."

"My sympathies," Nancy said.

"Yes, my husband. It was expected, so why didn't I buy a hat ahead of time?"

"These are what we have. I think this one might do for a funeral?" Nancy said, pointing to a gray velvet bonnet.

"No, no. I need black, of course. Silk, if you have it, although satin could be fine. I'd need some ornaments, too. Are these the only ornaments you have?" For over an hour they designed the woman's funeral hat. When the woman became overwhelmed with the choices she threw her hands up with a big, frustrated sigh—a tic Nancy had witnessed a few times before when Boston Brahmin women had deigned to shop at Miss Edwards. *These women teach each other how to behave,* Nancy thought with amusement, which soon was replaced with shame because this was a funeral hat they were designing. In the end, they designed three hats before settling on one the woman liked.

"I'd like to pick it up tonight, if that's okay," the woman said.

Nancy thought of the venison and potatoes. She could hurry home, make the pie in two hours, get it to Benjamin, and be back to the shop to work by candlelight. "I can have it done, but it will be very late. Maybe a brother can pick it up for you?"

"Will you take the payment in butter?"

"I'm not really in need of butter right now."

"Butter is what I have. There's an embargo! Won't you take it? The funeral is tomorrow. I'm really in a bind."

Nancy had too much butter from all these embargo-embarrassed women. She was tired of accepting butter, and she didn't believe that this woman couldn't pay. She just didn't want to pay. But perhaps Nancy could give the butter to Benjamin. "Butter is fine."

At her home on Back Street, Nancy baked the venison pie. She was pleased with her efficiency. She wrapped the pie in cloth and brought it to Benjamin, a good walk away on Belknap. The pie was still hot when she got there. The embargo was killing her brother—Benjamin was a cooper, and no one was buying his barrels. And then he got whooping cough, looking for work in the cold, which Nancy rightly blamed on the president's failed policy.

"What's this? I still have half of yesterday's pie," Benjamin said, kissing her on the forehead.

She felt the new roughness of his chapped lips on her skin. He hadn't been drinking enough water through this illness—his skin had turned from its usual wind-scraped red to a tombish gray. "You need two pies to battle whooping cough. And don't forget to drink."

"So you're an idiom-maker, too?"

He asked about her day, and she began by telling him about the woman demanding a funeral hat. She was happy to see through her brother's wheezing that he was just as annoyed as she was.

"She certainly wasn't acting like a fresh widow!" Nancy said. "And now I'm up all night making her a hat. What was I thinking?"

"Stop it!" Benjamin yelled. He coughed awhile, and she waited confusedly for him to finish. "You have to say no to women like this. You have to be cruel nowadays. No bartering— just take money. How else will you survive? And why are you making me pies? I can cook just fine. It's whooping cough."

They ate the pie together, and then she walked toward Back Street She hadn't told him that she had, in fact, said no to a woman earlier in the day, and that she still felt ill from the guilt. *Perhaps he was right,* she thought, looking at her shop, *but only about one woman.* Each case was different. She should have said no to the funeral hat, but it was too late: she'd promised the funeral hat this time. She ought to have started on it, but there was a bit of light left. Nancy would take time for herself, in honor of Benjamin. She went to the wharves to see the dead ships staggering in the icy water. Jefferson would be gone soon, and there was mounting pressure to ease the embargo. The senate was deliberating. *What silliness,* she thought, *to think you can affect Europe by strangling American commerce.*

She walked back in the dying light. On Union Street, she saw through the window of a café the woman who needed the hat that night. She was with friends, all in extremely fancy hats, laughing. Nancy never believed that this woman had a funeral, or if she did it was for a forgotten relative. She just wanted a new hat immediately—and how could Nancy say no to a sale? There was no way. The embargo had made Boston a city of well-dressed pirates, but Nancy would not join them. Tonight she would make the funeral hat by candlelight, and in the morning she would rise early to find the new entrepreneur on Prince Street and lend her what knowledge she could.

AUTHOR BIOS

Afua Ansong is a Ghanaian American artist who writes poetry and teaches contemporary and traditional West African dance. Afua's work has been read or performed at the 2016 PEN World Voices Festival, the Bronx Book Fair, Emotive Fruition, Poetry Street, and Weeksville Heritage Center. Her work can be seen or is forthcoming in *FOLIO, TAB, The Seventh Wave* and *Maine Review.*

Raymond Philip Asaph has published poems in *Poetry, The Humanist, Mississippi Review* and elsewhere. He lives near Ithaca, New York, and is about to Kickstart, and self-publish, his first book: *Four Short Stories and Ten Love Poems.* Find him on Facebook.

Joe Cottonwood grew up in Montgomery County, where he was drawn to the spell of the Appalachians. He built a house on the side of a mountain in La Honda, California, where he lives with his high school sweetheart (Walter Johnson High), raising children and grandchildren. He has worked as a carpenter, plumber, and electrician for most of his life. Nights, he writes. His most recent book is *99 Jobs: Blood, Sweat, and Houses.* joecottonwood.com.

MARIAN CROTTY is the author of the forthcoming short story collection *What Counts as Love,* winner of the John Simmons Short Fiction Award. She is an assistant professor at Loyola University Maryland and lives in Baltimore.

JOANNE ROCKY DELAPLAINE'S poems have appeared in *Poet Lore, Innisfree Journal, Beltway Poetry Quarterly, Gargoyle, International Poetry Quarterly, The Northern Virginia Review,* and elsewhere. She is a co-director of Café Muse, a monthly poetry-reading series sponsored by The Word Works, and a presenter at Split This Rock poetry festival.

DONELLE DREESE is a Professor of English at Northern Kentucky University. She is the author of three collections of poetry, *Sophrosyne* (Aldrich Press), *A Wild Turn* (Finishing Line) and *Looking for a Sunday Afternoon* (Pudding House). Donelle is also the author of the novella *Dragonflies in the Cowburbs* (Anaphora Literary), the ecofiction novel *Deep River Burning* (WiDo Publishing), and *Cave Walker* (Moon Willow Press). Her poetry and fiction have appeared in a wide variety of literary journals including *Blue Lyra Review, Roanoke Review, Louisville Review,* and *Quiddity International.* www.donelledreese.com

SUE EISENFELD is the author of *Shenandoah: A Story of Conservation and Betrayal* and a contributing author in *The New York Times' Disunion: A History of the Civil War.* Her essays and articles have appeared in *The New York Times, The Gettysburg Review,* and many other publications, and her essays have been listed among the Notable Essays of the Year in *The Best American Essays* in 2009, 2010, 2013, and 2016. She is a five-time Fellow at the Virginia Center for the Creative Arts and a member of the faculty at the Johns Hopkins M.A. in Writing and Science Writing programs. www.sueeisenfeld.com

RICHARD FARRELL is the Creative Non-Fiction Editor at *Upstreet*. He is a graduate of the U.S. Naval Academy and the M.F.A. in Writing Program at Vermont College of Fine Arts. His work, including fiction, memoir, essays, interviews and book reviews, has appeared in *Hunger Mountain, New Plains Review, Upstreet, Descant, Contrary, Connotation Press, Newfound* and *Numéro Cinq*. He teaches at San Diego Writers, Ink and the River Pretty Writers Retreat in the Ozarks. He lives in San Diego.

MATT FARRELL grew up in Sacramento and currently lives with his wife in Portland, Oregon. He received a B.A. in Film & Media Studies from Stanford and an M.F.A. in Creative Writing from the University of Oregon. He now attends medical school at Oregon Health & Science University, doing his best to write between rotations. His fiction and poetry have appeared in *Switchback* and *Arcadia*.

SAMANTHA LEIGH FUTHEY received her M.F.A. in the Creative Writing and Environment program at Iowa State University. She has poetry published in *RHINO Poetry, Superstition Review, The Fourth River, The Cider Press Review,* and forthcoming in *Alligator Juniper* and *Zone 3*.

E. LAURA GOLBERG emigrated from England to America at age 21. Her poetry has appeared in *Birmingham Poetry Review, RHINO, Gargoyle, Pebble Lake Review* and the *Journal of Humanistic Mathematics* among other places. Laura won first place in the DC Commission on the Arts Larry Neal Poetry Competition. She is preparing her first collection of poetry, *Drive-In Movie*.

MARY GRIMM has had two books published, *Left to Themselves* (novel) and *Stealing Time* (story collection)—both by Random House. She teaches fiction writing at Case Western Reserve University.

MELANIE HENDERSON, Washington, DC native poet, editor, photographer and publisher, is the author of *Elegies for New York Avenue,* winner of the 2011 Main Street Rag Poetry Book Award. An alumnus of Howard and Trinity Universities, she studied poetry at Howard University in Dr. Tony Medina's "Boot Camp" and at the Voices Summer Writing Workshops (VONA) in San Francisco, CA prior to earning an M.F.A. from Lesley University in Cambridge, MA. Her poems have appeared in *Beltway Poetry Quarterly, Drumvoices Revue, Jubilat, Torch, Tuesday; An Art Project, Valley Voices,* and *The Washington Informer* among others. She is a recipient of the 2009 Larry Neal Writers Award and received a 2013 Pushcart Prize nomination from Iris G. Press. She is a Founding Editor of *Tidal Basin Review* and Poetry Editor for Cherry Castle Publishing. www.dcelegies.com.

ALEX ANDREW HUGHES lives and works in Los Angeles. He splits his time between his training in clinical psychology and his creative pursuits. Sometimes, however, he does absolutely nothing, and he enjoys that time the most. His poetry has recently appeared in *Thin Air, New Plains Review, Firewords Quarterly,* and elsewhere.

RICHARD JONES is the author of seven books from Copper Canyon Press, including *The Correct Spelling & Exact Meaning.* Editor of *Poetry East* and its many anthologies, including *Paris, Origins,* and *Bliss,* he also edits the free worldwide poetry app, "The Poet's Almanac." A new book, *Pilgrim on Earth*, is forthcoming from Copper Canyon in 2018.

ROBERT P. KAYE'S stories have appeared in *Hobart, Juked, Dr. T. J. Eckleburg Review, Beecher's, Per Contra, The Los Angeles Review* and elsewhere, with details available at www. RobertPKaye.com. His chapbook *Typewriter for a Superior Alphabet* is published by Alice Blue Press. He facilitates the Works in Progress open mic at Hugo House and is the co-founder of the Seattle Fiction Federation reading series.

SANDRA KOHLER is a poet and teacher. Her third collection of poems, *Improbable Music,* (Word Press) appeared in May, 2011. Earlier collections are *The Country of Women* (Calyx, 1995) and *The Ceremonies of Longing* (University of Pittsburgh Press, 2003), winner of the 2002 Associated Writing Programs Award Series in Poetry. Her poems have appeared in journals, including *The New Republic, The Beloit Poetry Journal, Prairie Schooner, Slant, Tar River Poetry* and many others over the past 40 years.

LYNN MCGEE is the author of the poetry collection, *Sober Cooking* (Spuyten Duyvil Press, 2016), and two award-winning poetry chapbooks: *Heirloom Bulldog* (Bright Hill Press, 2015) and *Bonanza* (Slapering Hol Press, 1996). Her poems have appeared in many journals, including *The American Poetry Review, Southern Poetry Review, Ontario Review, Phoebe, Storyscape, Painted Bride Quarterly* and *The New Guard.* "Jupiter and Chaparral" is from her new manuscript, "Tracks."

LUCIEN DARJEUN MEADOWS was born in Virginia. His poetry has appeared in *West Branch, Hayden's Ferry Review, Quarterly West, Beloit Poetry Journal,* and *American Journal of Nursing.* An AWP Intro Journals Project winner, he has received nominations for the Pushcart Prize and recognition from the Academy of American Poets. Lucien lives in Fort Collins, Colorado.

SØREN G. PALMER teaches at the University of North Carolina at Chapel Hill. His work has been published in *Ecotone, Huffington Post, North American Review,* and shortlisted for the Flannery O'Connor Award for Short Fiction. He lives in Durham, with his wife and three dogs.

RICHARD PEABODY is a French toast addict and native Washingtonian. His most recent book is an omnibus— *The Richard Peabody Reader* (Alan Squire Publishing, 2015). He won the Beyond the Margins "Above & Beyond Award" for 2013.

CHARLOTTE PENCE'S first book of poems, *Many Small Fires* (Black Lawrence Press, 2015), received a *Foreword Reviews'* INDIEFAB Book of the Year Award and was a finalist for the Eric Hoffer Book Prize. The book explores her father's chronic homelessness while simultaneously detailing the physiological changes that enabled humans to form cities, communities, and households. Formerly a M.F.A. student at Emerson and staff reader for *Ploughshares,* Pence is currently director of the Stokes Center for Creative Writing at the University of South Alabama. She is also the author of two award-winning poetry chapbooks and the editor of *The Poetics of American Song Lyrics* (University Press of Mississippi, 2012). New poems have recently been published in *Epoch, Harvard Review,* and *The Southern Review.*

ANDREA POTOS is the author of six poetry collections, including *An Ink Like Early Twilight* and *We Lit the Lamps Ourselves,* both from Salmon Poetry in Ireland, and *Yaya's Cloth* from Iris Press. A chapbook entitled *Arrows of Light* is due out from Iris Press this year, and another full-length collection entitled *A Stone to Carry Home* from Salmon Poetry in 2018. Andrea received the 2016 William Stafford Prize in Poetry and three Outstanding Achievement Awards in Poetry from the Wisconsin Library Association. She lives in Madison, Wisconsin.

LIZ PRATO is fairly amazed that she wrote an entire essay about *The Descendants* without rhapsodizing at length about George Clooney. She is the author of *Baby's on Fire: Stories* (Press 53), and numerous essays and stories published by *Hayden's Ferry Review, Baltimore Review, Hunger Mountain, The Butter, Iron Horse Literary Review, Subtropics,* and more. She is the Editor at Large for Forest Avenue Press, and teaches at literary festivals from coast-to-coast. Liz is currently working on a linked essay collection that examines her decades-long relationship with Hawai'i through the prism of white imperialism. www.lizprato.com

SEAN SAM is a writer and member of the Navajo Tribe living in Maryland. His most recent works have been published in *Red INK, Bird's Thumb,* and *Two Cities Review.* seansam.com

ZLATINA G. SANDALSKA holds a doctorate in Russian Literature from University of Southern California and teaches Russian language, literature and culture at the University of California, Irvine. She has just completed her first novel, *Vomsk-348,* and is starting a second, set in the former Russian colony of Harbin, China. She loves to swim and ski (not at the same time).

MATTHEW SOCIA'S stories have appeared in *Tin House, Southern Indiana Review, CutBank,* and *Epiphany.* He has received a scholarship from the Bread Loaf Writers' Conference and an Emerging Writer Fellowship from the Writers' Room of Boston. He has an M.F.A. from Emerson College. Originally from northern Michigan, he now lives in Connecticut.

JULIA TAGLIERE is a freelance writer and editor whose work has appeared in *The Writer* and Hay & Forage Grower magazines; on the content website Buzzle.com; in various collections, including *Here in the Middle: Stories of Love, Loss, and Connection from the Ones Sandwiched in between, Candlesticks and Daggers—An Anthology of Mixed Genre Mysteries,* and the juried photography and prose collection *Love + Lust.* Her short story "Te Absolvo," was named Best Short Story in the 2015 William Faulkner Literary Competition. An active blogger, past finalist in Minneapolis' Loft Literary Center's Mentor Series Competition, and former student in DePaul University's M.A. in Creative Writing program, Julia currently resides in Maryland with her family, where she recently completed her M.A. in Fiction Writing at Johns Hopkins University.

MARY TAUGHER'S fiction has appeared in *The Gettysburg Review, Narrative Magazine, Edge, Prick of the Spindle,* and other literary journals. She lives in San Francisco where she is working on a collection of short stories.

KAREEM TAYYAR'S most recent book is *Magic Carpet Poems* (Tebot Bach). His work has been featured on The Writer's Almanac with Garrison Keillor, and in a wide variety of journals and magazines, including *Alaska Quarterly Review, Brilliant Corners,* and *The Santa Monica Review.* He holds a Ph.D. in American Literature from UC Riverside, and is a Professor of English at Golden West College.

JOSEPH ZACCARDI served as Marin County, CA poet laureate (2013-2015), and during his tenure published and edited *Changing Harm to Harmony: Bullies & Bystanders Project.* His poems have been published in *Cincinnati Review, Common Ground Review, Poet Lore, Spillway,* and elsewhere; his fourth collection of poems, *A Wolf Stands Alone in Water,* was published by CW Books in 2015.

www.ingramcontent.com/pod-product-compliance
Lightning Source LLC
Chambersburg PA
CBHW032006170626
46807CB00006B/2670